# THE HIRELING

*A Minister's Struggle for Position,
Recognition and Power Until
He Finds Redemption.*

## DENNIS H. DAVENPORT

WESTBOW
PRESS®
A DIVISION OF THOMAS NELSON
& ZONDERVAN

This is a work of fiction. All of the characters, names, incidents, organizations, and dialogue in this novel are either the products of the author's imagination or are used fictitiously.

WestBow Press books may be ordered through booksellers or by contacting:

WestBow Press
A Division of Thomas Nelson & Zondervan
1663 Liberty Drive
Bloomington, IN 47403
www.westbowpress.com
1 (866) 928-1240

Because of the dynamic nature of the Internet, any web addresses or links contained in this book may have changed since publication and may no longer be valid. The views expressed in this work are solely those of the author and do not necessarily reflect the views of the publisher, and the publisher hereby disclaims any responsibility for them.

Any people depicted in stock imagery provided by Getty Images are models, and such images are being used for illustrative purposes only. Certain stock imagery © Getty Images.

ISBN: 978-1-9736-3873-5 (sc)
ISBN: 978-1-9736-3874-2 (hc)
ISBN: 978-1-9736-3872-8 (e)

Library of Congress Control Number: 2018910554

Print information available on the last page.

WestBow Press rev. date: 09/14/2018

# CONTENTS

# CONTENTS

# INTRODUCTION

> I am the good shepherd: the good shepherd gives his
> life for the sheep. But he that is an hireling, and not
> the shepherd, whose own the sheep are not, seethe
> the wolf coming, and leaves the sheep, and fleeth:
> and the wolf cacheth them, and scattered the sheep.
> The hireling fleeth, because he is a hireling, and
> careth not for the sheep.
>
> —John 10:11–13 (KJV)

Though the main character in this story is fictional, it is my goal through this portrayal to deliver a powerful message to clergy and laity alike—the difference between a true shepherd and a mere hireling. The main character, Samuel Gashler, is a clergyman—a professional man of God. He's been to the right schools and has earned the required degrees to be called Rev. Samuel Gashler.

Rev. Gashler is a man tormented by personal demons. At the age of fifty, he struggles with himself over his lack of faith and commitment. He prays the right prayers and does the expected things in ministry without personal conviction or compassion. He's good at what he does, but he knows that much of it is hypocritical. He's been operating that way by the sheer momentum of his personality and abilities for many years.

Seminary had been a challenge. Many of the ideas he had learned at home and in church were challenged, but he managed to wade through it all, forming his own personal theology and approach to scripture. Through the years he evolved from an optimistic idealist into a somewhat cynical realist.

Ministry now is a profession based on personal achievement and promotion. He lusts for denominational recognition and acclaim. He's always climbing the ladder to greater heights. His highest goal is to pastor the largest and most prestigious church in his denomination—Ogden Memorial Church of Omaha, Nebraska. That would be the epitome of his personal dreams. He would finally receive the recognition and power he felt he deserved.

It's been a struggle. Rev. Samuel Gashler has pastored six churches over the years. Controversy has followed him to every one of them except one—that being Franklin Fellowship Church. But he was only there for eight months, and nothing controversial came to the forefront in that short of a time. Franklin Fellowship Church was a church of one hundred people located in a rural area of Iowa.

He felt it was beneath his stature and education to be there, but he had left his previous charge, Simpson Memorial Church in Kansas City, under a cloud of suspicion. Franklin Fellowship Church had only been a brief ministerial stop-over until something bigger would come along.

Rev. Gashler is married to the former Louise Thomas. Their relationship has been rather stormy and at times, cool. But in public they always pull together to project a semblance of love and harmony. Their marriage has produced two sons: Eric and Allan. Eric is now twenty-eight years old, married, and living in Iowa City, Iowa. Allan is twenty-three years old, single, and living alone in Davenport, Iowa. He is estranged from his father and wants nothing to do with church.

Rev. Samuel Gashler is called a pastor—a shepherd of the sheep. But is he? Does he love his sheep, or is he merely in it for position, recognition, and power? If he's not a true shepherd in the biblical sense, then what is he? Could it be he is more of a hireling?

# 1

# THE HEART ATTACK

It was a dreary and rainy morning as Rev. Samuel Gashler pulled into the parking lot at First Church of Sandusky. He hadn't been feeling well lately. He was quite sluggish and not up to his usual energetic self. Flu had been doing its thing, moving from person to person among his staff and congregation. Rev. Gashler wasn't about to let the flu get him down. He had too many meetings to attend that morning, a noon ministerial association luncheon, and five hospital calls to make that afternoon.

Margaret Ginsberg, the invariably prompt office secretary, would not be arriving until her usual time of a few minutes before eight. A person could set their watch by Margaret's promptness. She never wavered in her schedule. Rev. Gashler admired his secretary but felt he had to recommend to the church board that they gently retire this woman of seventy years. He wanted a younger person who would be computer literate and up-to-date on the latest office technology. Rev. Gashler felt Margaret was too slow as she tried to understand and do her job using their newest and latest computer. He liked Margaret and always got along with her, but it was time for her to retire. The church board had accepted his recommendation the night before, and he would have to tell her the bad news in a couple of hours. He wasn't looking forward to that nasty job.

Sam walked through the outer office, unlocked his door, and

proceeded into his inner sanctum. He loved his rather plush study. It was definitely the best and most spacious study he had ever had. There was plenty of room for all of his books and knickknacks. The church had provided him with a brand-new mahogany desk when he had taken the position as pastor at First Church four years earlier.

He loved and enjoyed his office, but after four years at First Church, he had experienced deep problems with some of the leadership. He was instrumental in encouraging several leaders to leave the church. He had no time for people who questioned his ministry. He only had time for those who adored and followed him unquestioningly. Rev. Samuel Gashler had set a pattern of church conflict almost everywhere he had gone. Many spiritual casualties had resulted from those conflicts.

He turned to his day planner calendar to see what he had scheduled and when. He knew it would be a busy day, as Wednesdays usually were. His board chairman would be meeting with him at 8:30 a.m. to discuss how to go about choosing new leaders to replace those who had recently departed from the church. He surely wanted to get his people in positions of power. Doing so would be crucial for his plans for First Church of Sandusky. He definitely didn't want anyone in leadership who would be less than supportive. No, that couldn't be tolerated.

His thoughts wandered past his Wednesday schedule to how he would break the news to Margaret Ginsberg. After all, she was a faithful member of the church. Her husband, Manfred, had been a successful farmer and was a big financial contributor to the church before his death eight years earlier. Her two daughters and their husbands were also members of the church. It would be like walking a tightrope for a while.

*What's going on?* he thought. Something was happening to him. His chest was tightening up, and his head was beginning to spin. He could hardly breathe as beads of cold sweat began to break out on his face. Nausea was rising up in his stomach. *What's happening to me?* A sharp pain shot down one of his arms. Sam cried out in panic, only to realize he was alone in the office. His first instinct was to call Louise. *Wait,* he thought, *she's away at a women's conference in Detroit.* He then started fumbling through his church directory for a telephone number of someone, anyone who would come take him home. He felt he needed to be home in bed. But before he could collect his thoughts, another sharp pain shot down his arm, throwing him to the floor. He drifted in and out of consciousness.

Rev. Gashler lay on the floor for what seemed like hours. He would be all alone, suffering a full-blown cardiac arrest, until Margaret Ginsberg arrived at her usual time of 7:57 a.m.

# 2

# The Family

Samuel Allan Gashler was born in Carthage, Missouri, to a lower
middle-class family. His father, Fredrick, worked two jobs to
support his family. His mother, Lois, stayed home to keep house
and raise the children. Sam had two sisters, Fredricka and Charity,
and a brother, Lonnie. Many of the household chores fell on him
because he was the oldest. It was also up to him to watch after his
younger siblings.

Fred Gashler had a drinking problem, which caused much
heartache and pain to the family. On many nights during his
childhood, Sam would wake up to hear his parents screaming and
hollering. One evening he remembered a neighbor had called the
police to come to the house and calm the storm. Sam was grateful
his father never got physically violent. The hollering and verbal
abuse to his mother was bad enough.

Lois Gashler was a religious woman. She was a faithful member
of the Elm Street Church in Carthage. Her parents were longtime
members of that church as well. She had married Fred in spite of her
parents' objections. Fred didn't want anything to do with religion,
although he professed a belief in God. He never wavered in his
position. And he always spouted the well-used phrase, "Churches
are full of hypocrites!"

Sam's mother always made sure her children attended the

church every time the doors were open. Elm Street Church was a good, solid traditional church. And even though there had been some problems over "liberal versus conservative" issues in the national denomination, Elm Street Church had been insulated from most of the controversy.

Sam loved his mother but only tolerated his father. He always felt he had to prove himself because of his father's drinking problem. They were known as the poor Gashler family from the wrong side of town. He overheard what people were saying about his family—his dad in particular. It made him angry at his father as well as at those who did the talking.

Young Sam grew up with a great deal of frustration, anger, and bitterness. He often wished his mother would become fed up and leave his father. He thought maybe she would find someone else, perhaps a churchman, and live happily ever after. Better than a divorce, he thought, wouldn't it be nice if his father died, relieving the family of the humiliation? Sam knew such thoughts were wrong, and he would feel guilty afterward.

Three days before his eleventh birthday, Sam's wish came true. He was called to the principal's office at the elementary school, along with Fredricka, Charity, and Lonnie, where they were told they needed to go home. Mr. Donner, the school's principal, volunteered to drive them the mile or so home to the north side of town. The four got out of his car and walked cautiously to the front porch of their house, where they were met by their mother, Lois. It was obvious she had been crying. Farther into the house they were met by young Rev. Jonathan McCray, their pastor of six months at Elm Street Church.

Lois told the four children to sit down and that she had something to tell them. With great hesitation, Lois tearfully told them their father had been killed in a one-car auto accident while driving home from Joplin the night before. Evidently Fred had been drinking and drove off the road into a patch of trees, where he hit one of them, killing himself instantly and critically injuring Bob

Turner, his drinking buddy and best friend. They were found by a farmer around ten o'clock that morning.

The three younger Gashlers broke out immediately into intense crying and could not be consoled by their mother or Rev. McCray. Young Sam sat in place on the sofa, obviously shocked and trying to take in all he had heard. His mind pulsated with the thoughts he had entertained for a couple of years concerning his father dying so his mother could be free of the torment. He didn't feel so good. Rev. McCray went to the sofa and sat down by Sam. He saw the good reverend's arm coming around him, but before it could be placed around his shoulders, Sam broke out into a run for the bathroom, where he just made it before throwing up.

Bob Turner died of his injuries a week later at the hospital. Bob's family blamed Fred Gashler for his death, therefore indirectly blaming all of the Gashlers.

Life got back to a semblance of normalcy after the funeral. Sam's brother and sisters seemed to adjust to being without their father. His mother cried from time to time for several months afterward. But Sam was different. His father's death changed his life. After all, he had wished his father would die, and it had happened. But now he felt a profound sense of guilt. He couldn't tell anyone. He would have to keep it to himself until his dying day. No one must know—especially not his mother.

Lois Gashler immersed herself into the church. She had always wanted to do more work at the Elm Street Church, but marriage to Fredrick Gashler hampered that ambition. She volunteered to work in the church office three days a week, taught a children's Sunday school class, and eventually became president of the Women's Christian Missionary Society. Lois sought to be a busy and contented servant of the Lord. All of her activities filled a void in her life. Soon after Fred's death, she made up her mind that she would not marry again. She felt life, for her, would be given to the Lord.

Sam worked hard after school, Saturdays, and during his summers at the local coop elevator. They liked him because he was industrious and reliable—more industrious than most teenage boys. Outside of owning a car and the costs involved with it, Sam saved as much money as he could during his junior and senior years of high school. He didn't know what he wanted to do with his life after graduation, but he knew he would need some money to do it.

His mother wanted him to become a preacher. She often said she wanted him to consider going into the ministry. Over the years Sam resisted it and avoided talking with her about it. But after his graduation, the pressure was on him to make some kind of a decision concerning what he really wanted to do with his life. He didn't want to work at the coop the rest of his life. He was above average academically in high school. Yet nothing really popped into his mind as to what he wanted to do with his life.

Larry Johnson and Billy Sampson talked about joining the navy. Billy ended up getting into trouble—something about stolen auto equipment. He left town in a hurry, traveled to San Francisco, California, and became a part of the drug culture. Larry was drafted into the army and served a tour of duty in Vietnam. He came back to Carthage and bought a service station but spent a great deal of time at the Veteran's Administration Hospital seeking help for his emotional problems.

That fall Sam enrolled at Southwest Missouri State University in Springfield. He still didn't know what he wanted to do, so he took a general course of study. After a painful bout with homesickness, he settled into the routine of classes, study, social activities, and work. The bulletin board in the school's administration building always posted jobs by local businesses. Sam pursued one he thought he might enjoy—work at Turner's Major Appliance Store. His job was to help with all deliveries and keep the store and its massive display windows clean.

College went well for Sam. He enjoyed the academic atmosphere. He took plenty of courses in philosophy and psychology. He thought he might become a psychologist. But he had a nagging thought his mother had placed in his heart over the years—that of going into the ministry. Becoming a psychologist would probably bring him more money than going into the ministry. Most preachers he knew from his days at the Elm Street Church lived quite modestly. He really wanted more for himself. Quite often he wrestled with what his mother wanted him to do.

He drank beer but was not into the hard stuff. He enjoyed some of the party life on campus, but girls were his weakness.

The thought of becoming a minister rested in the back of his mind all through college. He was headed for a degree in psychology and was hoping to go on in his education to become a clinical psychologist. His mother, Lois, stopped mentioning the ministry as he got closer to graduating from the university. Perhaps she gave up on him becoming a preacher. Regardless of that, Sam still felt pressure from somewhere about him going into the ministry, but the only times he went to church were when he went home on the weekends. In fact, he was always too tired on Sunday mornings in Springfield to get out of bed. Saturday nights were his time to unwind and have fun. Most weekends he wouldn't get back to his room until two or three o'clock in the morning.

College challenged Sam's faith. Most of what he had learned growing up attending church and Sunday school at Elm Street Church was torn apart in his philosophy classes. Science was also a great problem because of the teaching about evolution as opposed to what he had learned about creation from his mother and the church. Much of it muddied his belief system. As he approached graduation, he didn't know exactly what to believe on a variety of subjects concerning the Bible and his faith. He would lie awake nights thinking about his life, the future, his sinfulness, and his personal beliefs or lack thereof. He found it easier to lose himself in work and play. During his busy daylight hours, he didn't have to do much thinking, but the quiet of the night hours was something different. Sam tried to pray but felt God, if He existed, was too far away and that his prayers couldn't reach beyond his own mind.

# 3

## FOLLOWING GRADUATION

Graduation had come and gone. Sam continued to work at Turner's store, not knowing what he wanted to do. He didn't really want to go on to graduate school. He did have doubts about becoming a clinical psychologist. His enthusiasm for doing that had waned somewhat after he looked into it.

Sam decided not to make any immediate plans for further education. He felt he needed time to find himself and to work on paying off his college loans. Turner's was a great place to work. Kenneth Turner owned the store for thirty years and had built up quite a business in the Springfield area. Mr. Turner was pleased with Sam's loyalty, so much so that he offered him the position of store manager. This meant a substantial increase in pay. Sam was becoming more comfortable with his life in Springfield, but he still had a haunting feeling there was more.

Fall came and then winter. Sam enjoyed his social life. At first his circle of friends narrowed because most of his college buddies graduated and moved on. But he met and became friends with several of the single businesspeople in the downtown area. After becoming store manager at Turner's, he joined the Lion's Club and the local chamber of commerce. His circle of friends was expanding, and he truly enjoyed his popularity.

The ladies were taking notice of his popularity and good looks.

Sam loved flirting with them. He had little interest in dating just one. Sam dated several Springfield-area women.

Over the years Sam weaned himself of going home on the weekends to see his mother and family. His life was busier than ever since he had graduated from college, and he only went home on holidays and birthdays.

Fredricka, his oldest sister, moved to Muncie, Indiana, to attend Central States Bible College and Seminary. It was the closest denominational Bible school to her home, and she wanted to become a Christian education director at a church. Sam admired her faith and vision, but felt Fredricka was quite naïve. He also felt she could do much better monetarily by attending a secular university in pursuit of a secular job.

Charity, his second sister, was in her last year of high school in Carthage. She wasn't religious like Fredricka. Sam felt closer to her for that reason. He did find out that Charity was doing some heavy drinking and warned her about it. He didn't want her to end up like their father. Unfortunately, his admonitions went unheeded.

Lonnie, the youngest sibling, was a junior in high school. There was something different about him. He was not simply religious. Lonnie truly cared about people. Sam admired him for that but felt uncomfortable when he had to spend much time around him. For one thing, Lonnie used some words he wasn't used to—like "praise the Lord," "hallelujah," and "I love You, Lord." He knew Lonnie had something he didn't possess, but Sam didn't want anything to rock his boat. His social circle wouldn't understand it if he became a religious fanatic like Lonnie.

Sam's life was full as spring came and then summer. He loved his job. But there was one possible fly in the ointment. The Vietnam War was raging, and the draft lottery was in place. He was afraid his number would be chosen. Casualty reports were high. Three of his friends in college had gone to Vietnam. Two of them were dead. He hadn't heard any news about the other one. Sam knew he didn't want anything to do with military service.

As fall approached, Sam became more worried about his

situation. He seriously thought about escaping to Canada to evade the draft if his number came up. This would be most difficult because his father, Fred, was a hero at the battle of the bulge during World War II and received the Purple Heart. His mother was proud even though Fred was an alcoholic. For Sam to escape to Canada would be shameful to her. He knew his grandparents on both sides of the family would feel horrible about it too.

Sam went home for the Fourth of July weekend. He knew his family would be there to see the big Independence Day parade in downtown Carthage. He wasn't big on parades and crowds, but it always meant a great deal to his mother for all of her children to be with her for this great patriotic event. Fredricka would be home from Bible college. He hadn't seen her for almost a year because her finances limited her ability to travel. It would give him a chance to check up on Charity—and he would have to simply tolerate Lonnie.

Everyone said the parade was the biggest and best Carthage had ever produced. Of course, that was said every year by most. Sam was a little uncomfortable watching Lonnie march in the parade with two signs strapped to his front and back reading, "Jesus died for you!" and "Won't you live for Him?" Sam felt embarrassment and uneasiness sweep through his soul. But at the same time he admired Lonnie's boldness.

Every year the Veterans of Foreign Wars put on a giant fireworks display around ten o'clock that night. The entire town would turn out—with their expressions of oohs and ahs.

The Gashler family took their traditional spot near a towering oak tree. Sam found himself with Fredricka, engaged in a conversation about her life in Muncie. He really was interested. Sam and Fredricka had lost touch with one another over the months and were taking full advantage of the opportunity to talk as they walked a few yards away from the rest of the family.

Fredricka was enthusiastic about school and her part-time job as a nanny for one of the Bible college professors. She missed her mom and the rest of the family but said she had a sense of God's leading in her life.

Sam didn't know much about God's leading, but there was something about Fredricka's life in Muncie that appealed to him. Then she said something that really caught his interest. Fredricka mentioned the ministerial students were receiving deferments from the draft. He hadn't thought about going to Bible college and seminary as a means of evading the draft. Could that be his answer without escaping to Canada?

All the way back to Springfield Sam could think of nothing else. He loved his life and hated the idea of leaving it. But he felt his number was coming up in the draft, and he had to do something. It would certainly be a shock to his coworkers and friends. They knew him as someone who liked to party as a man about town. He had never indicated to them an interest in church or religion.

Lois, Sam's mom, would be surprised and raptured at the idea. His grandparents would be so proud of him too.

Sam found himself in the midst of a great battle during the last two weeks of July. He couldn't think of much else. For one thing, the ministry was a scary idea. His concept of ministers was formed during childhood attending Elm Street Church. They all were poor as church mice as well as somewhat stuffy.

He also had bad memories of what happened to Pastor Potter. For some reason, Pastor Potter hadn't gotten along with John Hawks, chairman of the elders. It went on like that for a year until Pastor Potter and his family went on vacation. Decisions were made in his absence. When he pulled up in front of the parsonage upon his return, he was greeted by the sight of all their furniture and belongings scattered out on the front lawn, and his key no longer worked in the front or back doors of the parsonage.

Going into the ministry was last on the list of things he wanted to do with his life. He had greater aspirations than to be a football to be kicked around by some self-righteous, power-hungry bigot like John Hawks. On the other hand, maybe the Vietnam War would be over by the time he was through seminary. Perhaps he would never have to really go into the ministry.

Sam made up his mind by August 1. He would go to Central

States Bible College and Seminary. He called the admissions office for the right papers, filled them out, and sent them back with the transcript of his high school and college grades. By the middle of August he received a letter welcoming him to Central States. Sam would have to be on campus and ready for classes by September 7.

He didn't have to tell all of his friends about his decision. It spread like wildfire as soon as he told one of them. "Sam Gashler, going into the ministry? You've got to be kidding!" was the immediate reaction. Kenneth Turner, his boss, tried to talk Sam out of it. He even offered him a substantial raise in pay. Oh, how Sam wanted to stay, but he had made up his mind and had to burn his bridges.

# 4

# SAM GOES TO BIBLE COLLEGE AND SEMINARY

S am had to take some Bible classes at the Bible college in preparation for his seminary work. The first year was a shock to his intellectual system. He was introduced to philosophy of the Christian religion taught by Professor Richard Andrews. Professor Andrews was quite conservative in his views on Christian doctrine, the virgin birth, and Christ's resurrection. Sam took it upon himself to set the good professor straight, which caused some heated discussions in and out of class. He often argued on the basis of what he had learned in his philosophy classes at Southwest Missouri State University. He never convinced Professor Andrews he was right, but they became good friends.

Sam got a job right away at McGrever's Department Store in the appliance department. The pay was only half of what he had earned at Turner's in Springfield, but a job was a job and it appeared to be one of the better part time jobs a full-time student could get.

Life on campus was dull compared to his life in Springfield. It was a challenge balancing classes, work, and study. There was little time for socializing. Sam was older than most of the Bible college students. He was looking forward to seminary the following year, where he would be with people closer to his age group.

He noticed one outstanding freshman girl in his Old Testament and music theory classes. At first, he didn't know if she noticed him or not. Some of the other girls fell all over themselves to be noticed by Sam, but this girl was different. He quickly found out within his first week that her name was Louise Thomas and she was from Dubuque, Iowa.

Louise was a shy and unassuming young woman from a pastor's home. Sam found out she was very "Christian" and was set on serving the Lord. He thought, *Out of all the girls on campus, why does this girl appeal to me so much?* Sam found himself thinking about her a lot, even though he dated a couple of the older girls at the seminary—that is, when time and money permitted.

He wasn't the same Samuel Gashler in Muncie, Indiana, as he had been in Springfield. He missed the parties, and he really missed being popular with the socialites—when he had the time to think about it. But his life in Muncie was taking on its own dynamics and good times. Gradually Sam's thoughts of his former life in Springfield faded to become a distant memory from a distant place.

Sam looked forward to being near Louise in class. He always tried to sit somewhere close to her. *Why, I feel like such a rookie when I'm around her!* he thought. *I get so nervous, and I never know what to say.* He wanted to ask her for a date, but the dean of women frowned on freshmen girls dating older male students. Dating her would have to wait until next year when she would be a sophomore—that is, if she would go out with him.

It was a long summer between his first and second years in Muncie. He was looking forward to entering the seminary and knew it would be three years of intensive study in theology, Greek, Hebrew, and Bible. His thoughts centered around his feelings for Louise. He didn't even know if she would be returning to Bible college in the fall. After all, they only had a casual relationship. At least she knew who he was, but he didn't know if she felt any more than that.

Sam made the trip home for the Fourth of July to see his mom and family. Fredricka went along to help drive and share the expenses. They planned to stay an extra week to help their mother celebrate her fiftieth birthday. That meant attending church at Elm Street Church for a Sunday service.

Sunday arrived sunny and hot in Carthage, Missouri. Lois Gashler was so pleased that all of her children were in church with her—just like when they were children. The second pew from the front was the family pew. Sam hated being that conspicuous to the rest of the congregation, who were sitting in the last six rows toward the back of the sanctuary. But Lois didn't give them much choice—not when they were growing up or on that particular Sunday.

Worship that morning had no surprises—consisting of invocation, scripture reading, hymn of praise, pastoral prayer, announcements, a choir number, offering, sermon, closing song, and benediction. There was one exception. It was Pastor Donald Frazier's message. He said little about the Bible or the gospel. His time was spent talking about social issues, the Vietnam War, and women's rights. Sam had not heard any of that in the past from the pulpit at Elm Street Church. Other pastors who graced the pulpit preached on justification, sanctification, and baptism. Those had always been sleepers for Sam, but Rev. Frazier interested him. He knew he had to talk to him before returning to Muncie.

Conversation at the Sunday dinner table eventually turned to Rev. Frazier's sermon. Fredricka brought up some fairly negative comments. "There are a few ministers preaching on those themes in some of our churches in the Indiana area. Personally, I find little in that type of sermon to feed my soul."

Sam had a different viewpoint altogether. "Freddie, I really enjoyed his message. He made some points I agree with—like US involvement in the Vietnam War. That's an issue straight out of the headlines, and I like what he said about getting out of Vietnam. I agree with him."

"Sam," Lois chimed in, "Pastor Frazier speaks a lot on political issues—almost every Sunday. A few people in our church like it, but most of us wish he'd preach about Jesus and what the Bible says."

"But Mom, these are important issues in our country today. I think Rev. Frazier is doing his God-given duty by speaking the truth on current events involving everyday life. True, he didn't use any Bible in his sermon, but he had some terrific thoughts. His command of the facts was marvelous. I also thought his using news articles to prove a point was excellent."

Charity was bored by the entire conversation and tried a couple of times to change the subject, to no avail.

After a little more dialogue between Sam and her, Fredricka finally asked, "Lonnie, what do you think of Pastor Frazier's message?"

Lonnie thought for an eternal second before answering the question. "Sam, I don't know much about politics or any of that kind of stuff, but I do know what the answer is to all of man's troubles. Praise God!"

Sam knew where Lonnie was going with his answer. "Jesus, isn't that what you're going to say?" Sam asked.

"You've got it!" Lonnie answered with enthusiasm.

"Well, I find that's a little simplistic."

Finally, Charity had had enough. "This conversation is going to Nowheresville!" Getting up, she went out on the front porch with her cup of coffee.

"Jesus died on the cross so that people would be at peace with God, with themselves, and with others. There can be no peace as long as He is rejected." Lonnie said it with such conviction— surprising Sam.

"Anyone want dessert?" Lois asked as she got up to head for the kitchen. "I baked your favorite, Sam—apple pie."

"The Vietnam War is an unjust war. There are thousands of students my age marching against it. I really admire them. They're making a difference." Sam couldn't help raising his voice to a higher pitch as he made his point.

"Pastor Frazier is a good man—and is very sincere. He believes what he preaches.

"I'll give him that. But I personally need sermons with spiritual depth."

"But Freddie, preachers like Frazier can change society and possibly the world." Sam felt embarrassed as he hit the table with his fist.

Lois came in carrying two pieces of pie. "Freddie, will you help me serve the pie and coffee? Lonnie, will you go get Charity?"

Sam's first year in seminary was most difficult. His thoughts and preconceived ideas about faith and theology were challenged on every hand. He came to a point where he didn't know what he believed. Several of his professors were theologically liberal and questioned everything about the Bible, the miracles, the virgin birth, and who Jesus is. Sam had been raised to at least semi-believe in traditional Christianity.

Even though his spiritual life was in shambles, he made progress with Louise that year. He finally procured enough nerve to ask her to go with him to the Fall Founder's Day Celebration, sponsored by the Central States Alumni Association. Louise enthusiastically accepted. What he didn't know was that she had had her eyes secretly on him most of the preceding year but her shyness prevented her from giving him any indication of how she felt.

Their romance blossomed from casual to serious in one school year. Sam actually hurt inside being away from Louise. He felt there wasn't enough time for them to be together. Seminary classes, study, and work at the store didn't give him much time during the week. They looked forward to Saturday nights and all-day Sundays to be together.

One Saturday evening, Sam and Louise were sitting in his car after going to see a play in Indianapolis. The car was in front of her apartment on the opposite side of the street. They were talking about their love for each other when Sam gave Louise a long, passionate kiss.

It thrilled her at first, but when it became apparent Sam was losing control, Louise said, "Stop! No, Sam! Don't do that! You're going too far!"

"But why? We love each other. We're going to get married someday. I don't understand." Sam knew better. His old life had kicked in.

"Sam, I love you—you know that, and I believe you love me. Don't you?"

He nodded his head sheepishly.

"For you to love me means you respect me—respect me enough to wait until we're married."

Louise never looked more beautiful and desirable to Sam than she did at that moment. Although he was embarrassed and ashamed of himself, he knew Louise was the woman he wanted to spend his entire life with.

Richard Nixon was elected president of the United States, and there was talk of peace with honor in Vietnam. Sam kept his ears open for any news about peace over there. If the war ended, perhaps he could leave the seminary. He found it hard and wanted to become a businessman—or maybe run for political office someday.

The Vietnam War didn't end while he was in seminary. Sam stuck it out, doing reasonably well in his studies. In fact, he studied himself into a rather liberal position on most issues—religious and political. That made for some rather heated debates between Sam and Louise. She didn't have a seminary education like Sam, but she had been taught well by her conservative preacher-father back in Dubuque, Iowa.

Louise graduated from Central States Bible College the same year Sam graduated from the seminary. That took place the last of May that year, with their wedding taking place the middle of June.

Sam had done some student ministry during his last year at the seminary, but being a full-time pastor in a church scared him to the core.

# 5

# OAK GROVE COMMUNITY CHURCH

The placement office at the seminary contacted Sam several months before his graduation, giving him a list of five Midwestern churches looking for pastors. Knowing there were others of his fellow seminary graduates looking for churches too, Sam rushed full speed ahead to get his resume out to the churches as soon as possible. He also sent copies to district superintendents of his denomination in most of the areas of the United States.

One day in April of that year, Sam received a call from the pulpit chairman, Peter Goddard, at the Oak Grove Community Church located three miles west of Simpson, Illinois. Mr. Goddard invited Sam and Louise to travel to Oak Grove. It would give them opportunity to meet and "kick the tires," as Peter Goddard so colorfully explained it.

Sam didn't like the idea of preaching at a country church. He wanted to go where the action was. But Louise was excited about the prospect of country living, a large garden, and the slower pace of life. Sam knew he would have to start somewhere. Oak Grove would be, he thought, the bottom rung on the ladder leading up to something bigger and greater.

Sam and Louise accepted the call to Oak Grove Church—a church of around fifty-five people in attendance for Sunday worship. Sam could always make a great first impression and tried hard not to preach anything controversial during his trial sermon. He used just the right amount of scripture and traditional theology to impress those Midwestern farmers.

The parsonage at Oak Grove would be their first real home together —their love nest, as they lovingly called it. It wasn't much to brag about with its peeling paint and cramped kitchen. But Louise loved it because she and Sam would be there together.

Peter Goddard, with Frank Lisson, another parishioner, drove his farm truck to Muncie to move Sam and Louise's belongings to Oak Grove Church. The newlyweds followed along in their car.

While Louise busied herself unpacking their things, Sam moved into his study at the church. It wasn't much—more of an afterthought study—located in a small room behind the altar. But it was all his and would be used for sermon preparation and study.

The people of Oak Grove Community Church were loving and friendly—except for one major personality. Her name was Elvyra Tabias Smythe. Tabby, as she liked to be called, never held office in the church and had no desire to. She had never married but owned the largest farm in the county. Everyone at the church fearfully respected Tabby and knew she was the controlling factor in its workings. In reality, nothing got done unless she was for it.

Tabby was not friendly at all. Her personality was no-nonsense and all business. Though she was not the church treasurer, nothing was spent without her approval. Though she had no position on the general board, no decisions were made without her consultation.

Tabby's commitment to the church was without dispute. But because of her intolerance and outspokenness, she had driven new members and prospects away from the church over the years. After all, it was her church, and she was the largest contributor. Her parents founded Oak Grove Church in 1891, and Tabby was now its oldest member, except for old John Flake, who occupied a bed in the Good Samaritan Nursing Facility in Simpson.

Sam had changed his mind about the ministry. On entering seminary, he was evading the draft and had little desire to actually go into it. But a feeling for the ministry had developed in his mind—especially during his last year in seminary. He didn't look at the ministry as a calling. It was a profession to him—a place to use his talents and to climb to a position of power within his denomination.

Along with ambition, Sam had a definite stubborn streak. Louise noticed it during their first month of marriage. Along with it was his need to control and be in charge. He hadn't shown much of that during their courtship—not to the degree she witnessed since their wedding and move to Oak Grove.

The mixing of Elvyra Tabias Smythe's matriarchal personality with Rev. Samuel Gashler's ambitious stubbornness and controlling spirit would be a formula for spiritual fireworks at the Oak Grove Community Church.

Nine months into his ministry, plans were made for his ordination. It would be a big deal for Sam and Louise. The event would take place at the Oak Grove Church, with denominational dignitaries from the district taking part. Oak Grove only had three elders. They would be in charge of organizing and carrying out the service, including who would do what and when.

The big day came—a beautiful, sunshiny Saturday in February. Sam's mom came from Carthage, along with Lonnie and two other women from the home church. Fredricka made the trip from Muncie, as well as Professor Richard Andrews from Central States Bible College and Seminary. Rev. Isaiah Smith, who was the District Superintendent of the Mid-American Conference, was to deliver the ordination address.

Charity had moved to Los Angeles, California, with the idea of pursuing an acting career. The family had not heard from her for several weeks, but they were not worried because she was known for her lack of communication. Sam felt she probably wouldn't have come anyway even if she had stayed in Carthage.

The ordination service went well. Louise was so proud of Sam. Her parents made the trip from Dubuque, Iowa, to be in attendance. It was important to Louise for her parents to witness Sam's ordination. Her father, Rev. Louis Thomas, didn't like Sam much and was quite vocal about it to Louise. She prayerfully wanted her dad to accept and even grow to love Sam. Unfortunately, it was not to be.

Rev. Thomas always said there was something about Sam Gashler he couldn't put his finger on—something insincere. Louise thought it was because Sam was taking Dad's little girl away from him. At best, Sam and his father-in-law learned to tolerate one another. The situation made for some tense holidays over the years.

Things went well with Sam's ministry during the first two years at Oak Grove. He was developing as a preacher, even though his sermons were, at times, a little too intellectual and political. The church tolerated young ministers like Sam over the years and were used to his kind of message.

Sam's problem at Oak Grove was not his message. His problem began when he crossed swords with Elvyra Tabias Smythe.

Tabby prided herself on her weekly call to worship at the beginning of every Sunday morning service. Sometimes she would do a religious reading, and sometimes she would read a religious poem. Sam tolerated it for two years but reached the breaking point when Tabby spent twenty minutes one Sunday doing her religious reading.

It was Tabby who complained when the service went one minute over an hour. That Sunday, with the long call to worship, two hymns, choir anthem, offering, and prayer, the service took fifty minutes, which gave Sam ten minutes to preach.

When it became apparent that he had little time, Sam made the decision to go ahead and spend his usual twenty-plus minutes preaching. After all, he had spent a good twenty hours preparing his oratorical masterpiece, and the congregation should hear every word of it. *Besides*, he thought, *today I must take my stand.*

To amplify the time restraint, someone years before had purchased and placed a rather large clock on the east wall of the sanctuary to Sam's right, where everyone could see it ticking away.

Noon came and went. One minute. Two minutes. Three

minutes, and then four. Louise could feel tension building around her. Sam was angry and couldn't have cared less.

Finally, as Sam was finishing his third point, Elvyra Tabias Smythe stood to her feet three rows from the front to proclaim, "Rev. Gashler, don't you figure you've preached long enough? After all, most of us have dinner plans, and some of us want to get to Sophie's Cafe before the crowd hits."

Stopped in his verbal tracks for a moment, Sam stood behind the pulpit, shocked by Tabby's audacity. He could feel the blood rushing to his face, turning it red with embarrassment and anger. Then something else kicked in way down deep inside of him—something he had little control over.

"Tabby—Miss Smythe—I'm not done with my message. Would you please sit down—and—shut up until I'm finished! Please!"

No one had ever spoken to her like that. It was obvious to all that she was stunned by Sam's confrontation. Following a moment in suspended animation, Tabby sat down in the pew she had occupied every Sunday all of her life.

Sam went on to finish his message, although it was apparent no one was really listening after the confrontation. As pastors had done since the beginning of Oak Grove Church, Sam took his place at the front door to shake hands with his flock. At first, he and Louise were frozen in time—wondering if the people would ever get up out of the pews to go through the reception line. Eventually most of them trickled out, going through the line like obedient soldiers. One thing was obvious—they all were uneasy and saddened by what had taken place that morning.

Tabby was the last person to leave the church building. She waited until all others had driven out of the parking lot.

"Rev. Gashler, you embarrassed me today. You talked to me like nobody ever has. I'm hurt and I'm mad!"

"Tabby, don't you think—"

"Let me finish what I'm saying. You've done pretty well here at our church the past couple of years, but I'm afraid your outburst today has changed all that."

Sam could feel the anger rising in his throat.

"What do you mean, Miss Smythe? What are you saying? Are you saying I'm through because I stood up to you—because I didn't let you run over me with your overbearing attitude?"

"Just let me say, Reverend, that I'll be here a long time after you've gone. People know me. But who are you? You're just another ego-driven preacher using our church as a stepping-stone to something bigger. It's obvious to me that you have little interest in our people. All you're interested in is being seen and heard. Furthermore, you're not that great of a preacher with all that intellectual and political mumbo-jumbo."

Tabby's words were like verbal torpedoes, sailing through the air hitting their intended target—cutting into Sam's spirit. He knew the argument was lost. She would never be beaten or tempered in any debate. It was at that moment he discovered who was head of the Oak Grove Community Church.

Monday came, but no one stopped by the parsonage—which was unusual. Farmers' wives would often bring a dozen eggs or some other produce to the Gashlers on Mondays as they had done for all the other pastors' families over the years.

Louise was extremely uneasy about the entire affair.

"Sam, you knew how she was. You knew she was a woman of great influence in the church. Things were going so well for us here. Why did you have to buck Elvyra Tabias Smythe, of all people?"

"Louise, there is room for only one pastor in this church. And that's me! She's been working behind the scenes against every proposal and plan I've presented. She's not on the church board yet she always knows and nixes everything—unless it's her idea. I'm tired of it and I won't—"

"Sam, please settle down!"

No one from the church came by the parsonage until Wednesday morning. Around 7:30 a.m. Sam and Louise heard a truck pull into their driveway. They had just finished breakfast and were sipping their coffee.

"Sam, it's Peter Goddard."

Opening the backdoor with a strong pull, Sam pushed open the screen door to let Elder Goddard's six-foot, one-inch frame into the kitchen.

"Hi, Pete, how are ya doing?"

"Well, Reverend, I'm doing good, but I need to talk to you a spell."

Sam anticipated that one of the elders would be dropping by. He also anticipated that an unofficial meeting without his presence had taken place somewhere in the parish.

"Reverend," Elder Goddard said nervously, "we're all real sad about the Sunday service."

"Pete, so am I. I wish it hadn't become necessary for me to stand up to her. Tabby has been a thorn in my side since I arrived two years ago."

"But Reverend, everybody fears and respects her. Don't you know that?"

Sam could tell Pete was upset and knew he represented the feelings of most of the church leadership. "Yes, I know that. But it's not right for her to be disrespectful to the pastoral office."

Peter Goddard was caught in the middle—a place he hadn't bargained for when he accepted the nomination for chairman of the board at the last congregational meeting.

"But Reverend, it's just the way she is. You're not going to change that. Most of us in the church love you and Louise. You've done well here. But if you don't apologize to Tabby next Sunday, things are going to happen none of us want."

"Apologize! You've got to be kidding! She should apologize to me!"

Sam could feel his face turning red. He knew Peter Goddard was seeing it turn red as well.

"Pastor, I'm telling you, this whole mess is going to blow up in your face. I don't want to see you and Louise get hurt. You've got to think of Louise."

"What do you mean by that? What can she do? She's an old lady who should have been put in her place a long time ago."

26

Peter thought for a moment, contemplating what he was about to say.

"What I'm trying to say is—we'll have to let you go if you don't apologize to Miss Smythe next Sunday."

"What! I can't believe it! You mean to tell me that the elders and leaders of this church are so weak as to allow this woman to run Oak Grove Church?"

"Sam!" Louise was afraid her husband had said too much. "Don't you think you'd better settle down? Don't you think we all should pray about this situation for a while?"

"I agree with Louise. You'd better get yourself under control. I'm afraid this has become a tempest in a teapot for both you and Tabby. She's not going to apologize to you—at least not until you do it first. Then there's no guarantee. Pastor, you can come out of this mess with the people's respect. But I'm afraid you're the loser if you don't humble yourself and apologize."

Peter Goddard excused himself and left, leaving behind a very disturbed pastor.

Sam spent many hours in emotional and spiritual agony the next few days. He lay sleepless most of the night hours leading up to Sunday morning. He spent his afternoons working on a sermon he titled "Pastoral Leadership." He felt this would be his one shot to set things straight at Oak Grove Community Church.

Louise tried to convince him not to preach on that subject. And she tried, to no avail, to talk Sam into apologizing to Tabby. She had been raised in a parsonage and knew the ins and outs of dealing with church people. By Friday night Louise was tired of arguing. She retired to the bedroom to pray—to give her husband and the entire situation over to the Lord. She found peace and slept soundly most of the night.

Sam hadn't found peace, but the course was set in his mind, and nothing could change it. By Saturday night his Sunday sermon was ready. He was ready to set it all straight.

There was tension in the air as people came for Sunday school and church. Tabby refused to speak to Sam and Louise, and most of the others spoke to them without emotion.

Tabby sent a message to Sam before the service saying she would not be giving the call to worship that morning. He felt it was a victory and it meant she was backing down. Little did he realize she had no intention of backing down. She was waiting for Sam's public apology that morning.

The worship service went smoothly without Tabby's personal touch in the call to worship. Sam used Psalm 100 as the call to worship and felt victorious in its use. Then time came for Sam's message.

"The title of my message this morning is 'Pastoral Leadership.' It is my desire in this message to help us all learn, see, and respect the pastoral office."

Immediately Louise sensed a growing tension in the room. She could hear people breathing deeper and with more bodily movement and paper shuffling in the pews. A tidal wave was about to hit her world, and there was nothing she could do about it.

Sam pressed on with his message without eye contact or much expression. His eyes were glued to the manuscript, and his right hand was clenched as if he were ready to strike. Five minutes went by and then ten. At the thirteen-minute mark, Louise could hear a commotion to her left. It was coming from Tabby's pew. Had she had enough? Was she getting ready to object to what she was hearing?

Louise had just thought those thoughts when, all of a sudden, Tabby stood straight up, stepped into the aisle, stomped to the back of the sanctuary, and rushed out the door.

The abrupt exit of Elvyra Tabias Smythe didn't slow Sam's message one bit. In fact, it appeared to Louise Sam was unaware Tabby had left the building. He had a message to deliver, and nothing was going to interfere with its completion.

After twenty-five minutes Sam brought his sermon to a close. He led the congregation, minus one, in a closing song and benediction. Louise and Sam took their usual place at the front door to greet the people as they left the building. Some of the congregants, however, escaped through the education wing into the parking lot to avoid facing any awkward or embarrassing moments. Some were too mad at the pastor to face him.

Louise spent an agonizing Sunday afternoon. Her head was splitting with a tension headache. Sam didn't seem to be too concerned about what had happened that morning. In fact, he felt he had done his righteous duty by setting the people straight on the matter of pastoral leadership.

No more than a couple of dozen words were spoken between Sam and Louise that entire afternoon. She kept expecting someone to call or arrive from the church leadership. Sam went to the bedroom to take a nap, leaving Louise lying on the couch nursing her headache. Her thoughts drifted back to their courting days in Muncie. How wonderful and carefree they were back then. It seemed like a million years had passed and they were living in a different world.

Sam slept like a baby for three hours that afternoon. Passing the couch on his way out the door to the church office, he noticed Louise was sleeping. He quietly tiptoed out the front door and headed down the sidewalk to the church.

An article had to be written for the monthly church paper, which would be published the next week. He didn't enjoy writing. It wasn't his strong point, but it was necessary to the workings of the Oak Grove Church because the pastor had always published one.

It was growing dark when Sam saw a pair of headlights in the parking lot. A new Buick was pulling up outside the church. He knew who it was, and he knew, of all the people at Oak Grove Church, Frank Anderson would be on his side.

Sam met Frank at the front steps of the church and led him into the pastor's study. After both men were seated and after some small talk, Frank began to share his thoughts.

"Pastor, I thought your sermon was right on. Tabby and the leaders of our church should have heard that message years ago. That woman has held Oak Grove back for years. It took courage for you to speak out. You've got my full support. And I just want to say—"

"God bless ya, Frank. That means a lot to me and Louise."

"Well, you two mean a great deal to Susan and me. You've always been there for us. And I just want to say that we're going to be there for you."

With that statement, Frank and Sam wrapped their arms around one another in a giant embrace.

"Frank, how do you think the rest of our people are taking all this? I've got to tell you that Tabby has implied to me that I'll be fired over this. And Elder Pete Goddard told me I needed to apologize to her or I'd probably lose my job. But I can't apologize for taking a stand I feel strongly about."

"Pastor Sam, so many of them are like sheep. They don't like conflict, and they don't like confrontation. That's why that old ... uh, that old woman has run the church all these years. They're afraid of her."

"I know. Isn't it sad?"

"It sure is. I don't know how this will turn out, but you've got my support. I know of two other families who feel the same way."

"You mean the Brenners and Taggerts?"

"Yes, I think they're fed up with Elvyra Tabias Smythe."

Sam was amused by the way Frank had spoken Tabby's full name—as if he had just tasted a sour lemon. He was encouraged by what Frank said about the Brenners and Taggerts. The more people on his side, the less power Tabby would have.

"Frank, could I get you to talk with Bob Brenner and Jake Taggert to see how fed up and how committed they really are to seeing this thing through?"

"Sure, Pastor. What do you think about having a meeting at my house tomorrow night? I think they'd come."

"Hmmm, well, as long as it doesn't leak out to the rest of the church."

"Oh, I think we can meet without a problem. My farm house

sits quite a ways from the road. We'll have a chance to talk and see what can be done."

"Thanks, Frank. I really appreciate your help."

"No problem. I'll call you about the meeting sometime in the morning."

The two men walked to Frank's car and shook hands. Sam watched the Buick drive out of the church parking lot.

Monday morning arrived with an inch of snow on the ground. It wasn't unusual for there to be that kind of snow in Illinois during February. Louise was still nursing her headache but said little about it to Sam. She knew he had much on his mind and didn't need to be worrying about her.

They had just finished breakfast when the phone rang. It was Peter Goddard on the other end. Louise recognized his voice when she answered it.

"Sam, it's for you. It's Peter Goddard."

"Good morning, Pete. Cold and snowy, isn't it?"

Louise was too nervous to listen. She walked into the living room out of earshot. Sam listened as Elder Goddard explained the disappointment he and the church leadership shared about how their pastor was handling the mess.

"Reverend, we've decided to have an emergency board meeting Tuesday night—tomorrow night at eight o'clock. I'm calling on you to be there. We've got to get this all settled for the good of the church."

"Pete, you know my position and how I feel."

"Yes, Reverend, I do. But you've got to understand my—our position. Tabby is the main sustainer of this church. Her money—"

"That's it, isn't it? It's her money! You're all afraid she'll stop giving and withhold her finances."

"That's part of it, but I won't discuss it anymore over the phone. We'll hash it out with you at the meeting. Goodbye."

Sam hadn't felt uneasy until that phone call. The prospect of confrontation and a fight both exhilarated and frightened him. But in his mind, he was righteous and would fight this thing through—for the good of the church, of course.

Around noon that day, the phone rang again. It was Frank Anderson. Sam took the phone from Louise and said, "Hi, Frank. What's up?"

"The others—Brenners and Taggerts—are on board. We'll meet tonight. Okay?"

"Okay, Frank. What time?"

"Let's make it eight o'clock."

"That'll be fine. Oh, by the way, do you know about the emergency board meeting called for tomorrow night?"

"Yeah, well, yes I do. Jake Taggert told me about it when I called him this morning. He's on the board, ya know. But I'm planning on being there too. I'm not a board member this year, but any church member can come and voice an opinion. But only board members can vote."

"Okay, Frank. That'll be good. I hope the Brenners will be there too. And I hope we'll have enough firepower to make a difference. We'll see ya tonight at your house."

Louise didn't want to go to the clandestine meeting at the Andersons, but Sam strongly insisted she be there to offer him support and to show the others they were united. In actuality, Louise didn't feel supportive of her husband. She felt hypocritical about making a united front. Yet she knew she had to stand by her husband regardless of whether he was right or wrong.

Sam was excited all afternoon about the Monday night meeting. Louise could hear him singing from time to time and wished she could share in his enthusiasm. But she had witnessed similar things happen to several colleagues of her father. She knew a full-blown church fight usually ends in forcing a pastor to move. Sam was determined, idealistic, and ambitious. There was something down deep inside of Sam—something hidden—that caused Louise great concern. It was a part of him he didn't want anyone to know or see—not even his wife.

Frank and Susan Anderson lived with their three children in

a large, newly redecorated and restored old farmhouse. Driving up the long lane to the house, Sam and Louise noticed two other cars parked in front of the house. The Brenners were just walking inside the front door as the Gashlers drove up. The Taggerts were obviously already inside.

Upon seeing their arrival, Frank Anderson rushed out to greet them in his husky way. After a few words of small talk, he ushered Sam and Louise into his living room, where the others had already gathered.

Frank reserved a place of honor for the Gashlers on plush chairs in front of the large fireplace. Louise was chilled to the bone, so the heat felt good.

"Rev. Gashler, would you offer a prayer before we begin?" Frank wanted everything to be proper and religious. He believed prayer by the pastor would set a Christian tone to the meeting.

"Certainly, Frank. Our most gracious and holy God, we come to You tonight, asking for guidance and wisdom. You, oh Lord, are the mighty God of the universe. You rule the earth and skies. Please shine upon us Your favor. May what we decide here tonight be immersed in Your wisdom and will and may You move on our behalf, changing the minds and hearts of those who oppose us. Amen."

Frank launched into the dialogue immediately. "You all know why we're here—so I won't rehash what happened a week ago or what happened yesterday. It's obvious our church is having a leadership crisis. We must ask ourselves the question as to who will lead us—Rev. Gashler or Elvyra Tabias Smythe."

"Frank, can I say something here?"

"Sure, Pastor, go ahead."

"Louise and I are troubled by the conflict in our church. I didn't wish it nor do I promote it. But a conniving, controlling, and spiteful old woman has thrust it upon us. I believe Tabby is running and will continue to run the Oak Grove Community Church. I personally am offended by the fact that she is the unelected head of our church."

"Amen to that, Reverend!" Jake Taggert broke in. "She's been offending me for years, but there was never a pastor, until you, who would stand up to her. I applaud you for that."

"Thanks, Jake."

"But what can we do about it?" was Emily Brenner's question. "I mean, there are only three families—four with the pastor's. The rest of the church is either afraid of Tabby or is solidly on her side."

Sam thoughtfully said, "Emily, our only weapon is to stand firm and make our voices heard. If we do that, we may see some of the others come over to our side."

Emily Brenner was uneasy about the prospects of causing a split in the church. She was raised, baptized and married at the Oak Grove Church. She had cousins she knew were pro-Tabby. But her husband, Bob, was firmly for what the pastor was doing. She knew she had to go along too.

The evening adjourned with a unanimous decision to attend the board meeting Tuesday evening. Sam was almost giddy about their decision. Louise thought his mood was strange in light of the fact that he could lose his first pastorate—to something as stupid as a call to worship.

The church library was packed Tuesday night as Sam and Louise came in the door. Two seats had been reserved for them across the long conference table from Elvyra Tabias Smythe. The board members occupied all other seats around the table, with curious and supportive church members filling the seats around the outside of the room. There had not been a large crowd like that for any board meeting at Oak Grove Community Church, but the word had gotten out and the battle for the church was about to begin.

Board Chairman Peter Goddard brought the meeting to order and offered up a short prayer that all things would be done decently and in order.

"It's unfortunate that this emergency meeting had to be called. It's painful for all of us to see the deep rift that has come up. If we don't get something settled tonight, I'm afraid all of this will get out of hand. With that having been said, I turn to our pastor, Rev. Gashler, to say a few words from his point of view."

"Thanks, Elder Goddard. I'm also pained by the events of the past two Sunday mornings. I didn't and I don't take pleasure in taking a stand against Miss Smythe. But I feel there is a leadership crisis in our church. On the one hand you have a pastor who is well-schooled in the affairs of church—one who has an idea and feel for where the church should go. On the other hand, you have a woman who has never held an office in the church nor has she wanted to, who basically runs the church through intimidation. Nothing, I mean nothing, is accomplished around here unless Miss Smythe—Tabby—is for it. I believe this leadership crisis is holding the church back."

With that, Sam sat down next to a very uneasy Louise.

"Thank you, Pastor. Now we turn to Tabby."

"I'm not as eloquent as Rev. Gashler. But I want you all to know that I love you—and I love Oak Grove Church. My folks founded this church. They gave the land for this building. I was born in this community. I came up in the Sunday school. I was baptized in this church. My roots are here. You all know who I am and you know my commitment to this church. I did not intend to cause stress for the pastor, but obviously, his trouble with me goes back farther than two Sundays ago. Obviously, he has trouble with my commitment to this church. That's his problem—not mine!"

Sam could feel anger rising up within. He knew confrontation with her would be useless. She would not bend nor even try to understand his point of view. Tabby would settle for nothing less than a full apology—a full public apology. That was something he couldn't do. His cause was righteous. Hadn't the people heard his sermon? Hadn't they understood his message?

Tabby went on. "Reverend, you owe me an apology. You owe this church an apology, not just for what you said to me. You owe it an apology for your high-sounding messages us country folk have a hard time following. And your politics coming from the pulpit rub many of us the wrong way."

"Chairman Goddard, can I say something in defense of the pastor?" Frank Anderson couldn't hold back any longer.

"Pastor Gashler has always been there for our family—through a couple of crises, as you all know. Susan and I love both Rev. Sam and Louise. I don't know much about theology or preaching, but I do know Rev. Sam is a good man. And I also know that Miss Smythe has a lot of power in our church. I, for one, don't appreciate her running the church. That's all I've got to say."

Tension exploded in the room. No one from the congregation had ever spoken about her the way Frank Anderson had. He made some people think, but he also made others mad. It was difficult for Chairman Goddard to bring order back to the meeting. Accusations were flying around the library unabated.

"Rev. Gashler is splitting our church!" someone yelled out.

"Who does Tabby think she is? The pastor's right in standing up to her," another protested.

"I think the pastor's got to go!" several people shouted.

Pete Goddard had had enough of the chaos. "Sit down and shut up—all of you! Let's bring order here! Let's start acting like Christians again! Please!"

Louise couldn't believe the yelling and screaming she was witnessing—coming out of normally civil people. She felt ashamed and wanted to go home—not to the parsonage. She wanted to rush home to Dubuque, Iowa, and into the loving arms of her precious mom and dad.

After a short break, the meeting resumed with Tabby's supporters saying a few words on her behalf. Then it was Jake Taggert's turn to speak.

"Miss Smythe, don't you think it's time you loosened your grip on our church? Pastor Gashler is only trying to help our church by casting a vision. Actually, what happened two Sundays ago was only a symptom of your trying to keep control. I think you were out of order interrupting his sermon. I think you owe him an apology."

"What do you mean, loosen my grip!" Tabby interrupted.

"I mean that you work behind the scenes getting your way

36

in every area of our church. Remember the sign in front of the church? Almost everyone thought it was a great idea. The board went so far as to set up a committee. But then you heard about it and you started weaving your web—drawing people into your net. It wasn't long before most of the board was against it. You do that all of the time. I'm personally sick of it!"

Tabby bristled at Jake's last statement. "Well, we don't need a sign out front. The one on the church building is good enough. My father made it years ago. It just needed to be repainted. Most of our people—"

"Yeah, most of our people are too timid to stand up to you!" Frank Anderson abruptly interrupted.

Chairman Goddard allowed discussion to follow—much of it negative against Rev. Sam Gashler. It was apparent to Louise that Sam's side was losing. She couldn't see much support for her husband, other than the Andersons, Taggerts, Brenners, and possibly two other families. She hurt for Sam, even though he seemed stimulated by the entire mess.

"Ladies and gentlemen," Pete Goddard broke in. "I propose that this board meet in a closed-door session—probably tomorrow night—to decide what we should do as a church. We've heard the complaints from people on both sides of the issue. I believe we can formulate a decision based on what we've heard tonight."

After a short discussion, the proposal was affirmed. A short prayer followed and the meeting was adjourned.

The church board would be meeting Wednesday night without Pastor Gashler and his people in attendance—except for Jake Taggert, who was a board member. Louise knew she would be packing but felt relief the ordeal would be over soon.

None of this appeared to concern Sam. He seemed aloof from the whole ordeal. Louise was irritated by his cavalier attitude. All she could think about was where they would go. And of course, there was that other little matter she hadn't told Sam about.

Wednesday went by at a snail's pace for the Gashlers. Sam spent his day in the church office preparing his message for the next

Sunday. Louise spent her day nursing a tension headache and an upset stomach. In a few hours they would both know their future or lack of it at Oak Grove Community Church.

That day Sam received phone calls from the Andersons, Taggerts, and Brenners, giving him their thoughts on the previous night's meeting. All of them said they would leave the church if he was fired.

The telephone rang at the parsonage around 10:05 p.m. It was Pete Goddard.

"Rev. Gashler, the board meeting is over, and I need to give you the results. I'd rather not wait until morning even though it's late. Mind if I stop in?"

Sam noticed the cars in the church parking lot and saw the lights on in the church library. In a few minutes he and Louise would know their fate.

Chairman Goddard was obviously nervous about his task as Sam opened the door to let him in.

"Come in, Pete. Long meeting, wasn't it?"

"I guess it was. We had lots of stuff to talk about and rehash."

"Come on in and sit down. Can I get you something?"

"No, Reverend. I want to say my piece and then go."

Louise was listening from the far side of the living room. She could tell from Pete's demeanor that the news wasn't good.

"Okay, Pete. Let's hear it."

"Reverend, I've tried to be a supporter of yours from the beginning. I believed in you and have backed you when others in our congregation were grumbling about you. But I'm afraid you lost me when you dug your heels in and refused to apologize to Tabby Smythe. I know you think you're right. But right or wrong, we're a small country church here and can't afford to lose Miss Smythe's support. We've been functioning as a church family all these years and don't want that upset. You, my friend, must realize the dynamics of our church and support it. If you can't do that and apologize to her, then you must go."

Sam lost his cockiness for a moment. "Pete, what are you saying?"

"I'm saying, Pastor, the board voted to have you removed if—if you don't change your mind and apologize to Tabby and to the congregation—publicly. If you don't do that, there are two options. You can resign and our board will write a good recommendation for you. Or if you choose not to resign, we'll fire you without a recommendation at all."

"You do realize there are three families who will leave the church if I leave, don't you?"

"I figured that, and I figured you weren't discouraging them any. What kind of a minister are you anyway? I think it's horrible how you've—how you've—oh, I'm getting too upset."

"Sorry you feel that way about me, Pete, but I can't budge on this. You'll have my resignation in the morning."

Louise couldn't believe how resolutely and confidently Sam spoke of resigning. She was torn up inside. How could she ever follow him into another pastoral situation? How could he ever feel up to taking another pastorate?

As promised, Sam wrote his resignation as pastor of Oak Grove Community Church and delivered it to Chairman Goddard. Sam was then informed that he and Louise could live in the parsonage until another position was offered to him or until Oak Grove Church called another pastor. Sam would receive two months' severance pay but could no longer preach or perform any other pastoral duties at Oak Grove.

Sam got busy contacting the district superintendent as well as churches he knew that were looking for pastors. Louise, on the other hand, was devastated by her Oak Grove experience and was secretly hoping Sam wouldn't find another church. She longed for a life of their own—one without tension or church politics. But as the days went on, the chances of that happening became more remote.

Then there was the little problem—that little blessing. After the dust settled from the church problems stemming from Sam's resignation, Louise began looking for the right time to tell him.

Saturday morning came, and she felt she would have Sam's full attention.

"Honey, I have something to tell you. With all the other things on your mind the past two weeks, I didn't want to burden you."

"Burden me? What's wrong? Are you sick? What's—"

"Sam, you're going to be a daddy! I'm pregnant!"

Sam sat in his chair for a moment with his chin drooping toward his chest.

"Honey, did you hear me?"

It appeared to Louise he was weighed down by the announcement.

"Oh, Louise. The timing is lousy."

"But I thought you'd be pleased and—."

"I am pleased. I'm happy for us, but the timing is lousy. Our future is so uncertain. I just wish things were more secure."

# 6

# CRESTVIEW FELLOWSHIP CHURCH

Crestview Fellowship Church of Des Moines, Iowa, was a suburban congregation of around two hundred families. Sam was given a glowing report and recommendation for the Crestview Pulpit Committee by his district superintendent back in Illinois. After a trip to Des Moines and a tryout sermon, he was called to be their new pastor.

Crestview was a twenty-seven-year-old church at the time of Sam's call. Rev. Daniel Powers was the founding pastor and had been its only pastor until his retirement six months before Sam and Louise arrived.

Sam was excited about the prospect of being the pastor of a city church. He felt his talents had been wasted on those hick farmers back in Oak Grove. City people would be more sophisticated and able to understand what he would be trying to accomplish.

Louise was glad to be away from Oak Grove. After the falling out, some of the people shunned her and Sam. It felt good to have a brand-new start with church people who respected and followed Sam's leadership—for a while at least, and forever at best.

The people of the Crestview Church had purchased a building from a Baptist congregation twenty years earlier—a seventy-five-year-old building that would seat six hundred people comfortably. Sam was excited about its potential for growth. The present attendance for a good Sunday service was around three hundred people. He had visions of filling the sanctuary to capacity.

While Sam launched into the work of the church, Louise busied herself preparing the house and getting ready for the new baby. Life was good, and she was happy being the wife of a respected city minister. The elders and church board seemed to be behind Sam 100 percent. She felt, at the time, that she could live in Des Moines, Iowa forever.

Rev. Samuel Gashler was developing his skills in leadership—or was it manipulation? He grew to know and use church politics to get his way. He persuaded some of his leaders to follow him blindly. Others he made to feel important and get on board, even when they originally objected. A handful of the leaders—the power-ites, as Sam called them—objected to most of Sam's proposals as time went on. But they were a small group, and he simply worked around them. They were the older leaders who had founded the church with Rev. Daniel Powers.

Sam admired Daniel Powers. He became acquainted with him through conventions and conferences. Sam felt they would be great friends since Rev. Powers and his wife, Mabel, were remaining in Des Moines as members of the Crestview Church. During the first six months Sam counseled with Rev. Powers. But it stopped when Rev. Powers tried to temper Sam's grandiose vision for the church. He told Sam he felt his ideas were self-centered and not Christ-centered. This put an immediate wall up between the two ministers.

Eric Samuel Gashler arrived on September 9 to Rev. Samuel and Louise Gashler. Mother and son were both fine. Father was a little worse for wear but survived the ordeal. The Crestview Fellowship Church was excited about the new baby. There had never been a baby born to a pastor of the church. Both Rev. and Mrs. Powers were forty-five years old when the church was founded. The older women, especially, were overjoyed with Baby Eric.

Rev. Samuel Gashler was growing in prominence within the Des Moines community. He was asked and accepted a position on the Mayor's Youth Council. He was elected vice president of the Lion's Club, and one of the local television stations invited him to participate in a program called *The Clergy Speaks*, aired on Sunday mornings.

Sam felt his power growing and reveled in it. Louise, on the other hand, was witnessing a change in Sam—a change she didn't like. He was becoming more prideful and less tolerant of other people's opinions. She felt an expanding wall between the two of them. She loved their home and church, but she hated whatever was causing Sam to change. She tried, on one occasion, to explain how she felt, but Sam denied he was changing and shut down the conversation.

Sam's ministry at Crestview went smoothly, for the most part, during the first five years. The Sunday morning attendance expanded from three hundred to over five hundred during those years. Most of the people were pleased with how things were going. But some of the older leaders of the church didn't like Sam's style of ministry. In fact, they didn't appreciate his in your face, love it or leave it type of leadership. They found him egotistical and unyielding. Even though the church had not been as prosperous as it was under his leadership, they were turning more and more to Rev. Daniel Powers.

Crestview's church staff consisted of Sam as senior pastor, Rev. Tony Parks as youth pastor, and Brenda Leighton as office secretary. On the surface the staff seemed to get along. But down deep inside, Rev. Parks resented Sam. He had known him at Central States Seminary but had felt he was not a sincere person. He believed there was something hidden within Sam. But Rev. Gashler was his senior pastor. He would do his best to work under his leadership— at least for as long as he could.

Because of Sam's success in growing Crestview, he was being offered speaking engagements far and wide in his denomination. This left Louise and young Eric alone. She needed Sam at home, but he was hardly ever there between his pastoral work and his frequent speaking engagements. Louise entertained thoughts of leaving him but fought them off. Divorce was a word her parents taught her never to use. She felt guilty even having a passing thought about it.

Trouble was brewing at Crestview even though Sam was elated by all of the open doors and opportunities. He was getting his way on most of his proposals. Things were hopping, and he was thinking about adding at least two new associate pastors. That would free him to pursue even more opportunities in the community and denomination.

What Sam didn't know was Rev. Tony Parks and Rev. Daniel Powers were meeting secretly to discuss their feelings about him. Their first meeting took place at Rev. Power's home. Rev. Parks had called the meeting, setting up the appointment.

"Come on in, Tony. Sit down. Mabel, get Tony and me a cup of coffee. How are things going at the church?"

"Well, that's what I'm here to talk to you about, Pastor Powers. On the surface things are going great."

"On the surface, you say?" Rev. Powers felt he knew where the conversation would be going.

"Yes, on the surface. It's just that I have these thoughts and feelings about Rev. Gashler. I mean—well—I've tried to examine my own heart and motives. I don't think I'm jealous of Sam. It's just that ..."

"It's just that you feel he is an insincere opportunist. Right?"

Shocked by what had just come out of Rev. Powers's mouth, Rev. Parks said, "Well, yes. How did you know?"

"Tony, I've had those thoughts too. And I've searched my own heart. I'm not jealous of his success. I applaud it—or at least, at first, I did. But down deep inside I feel Rev. Gashler is power-hungry and self-centered. I told him that a while back. We were friends until then. Now he won't speak to me when I speak to him. He won't even return my phone calls."

"There's tension between Sam and me too. Nothing's been said, but he knows I'm not on board with everything he does."

"Tony, there are others in our church feeling as we do. Most of them are people who helped me start Crestview and have been with me from the beginning. They wonder about Rev. Gashler's motives and ambitions."

Rev. Parks seemed surprised and relieved by what he had heard. "Rev. Powers, what can we do about it? I mean, he's so popular, not only in our church, but in the community as well."

"Son, the only thing we can do is keep our eyes open—and pray. I pray God will change his heart and make him humble. I pray for our church—that our church will not be harmed by this—by this hireling."

"Hireling, Rev. Powers?"

"Yes. I'm referring to what our Lord said in John 10:11–13. When you get back to your study, look it up."

Sam heard things through the grapevine about certain people being disgruntled in his church. He dismissed them as being "power-ites"—as he called them. Things were going very well at Crestview, he felt, and his hand-picked leaders would eventually overpower his opposition. In the meantime, he would stay the course and ignore those who stood against him.

Louise wanted another baby the second year after Eric's birth, but she didn't become pregnant until their sixth year at Crestview Fellowship Church. She knew in her heart the reason she hadn't become pregnant. It was the overwhelming stress she felt as well as the fact that Sam was either gone or not interested most of the time.

Their second son, Allan, arrived on a cold and blustery Iowa night of January 14. Eric was happy to have Allan and looked forward to his role as an older brother. Louise thought it was because Eric didn't have much of a relationship with his father that he attached himself so much to his younger brother.

Louise was a silent sufferer. She seldom shared her feelings with Sam. Most of the time it was due to his pressing schedule and preoccupation with his ministry. A deep resentment was growing in her heart against her husband. Louise couldn't help feeling she and her babies were barely on Sam's priority list—if at all.

In spite of a small but slowly growing number of dissidents in the church, Sam's ministry and influence were growing. He loved the feeling of fame and power. By their sixth year at Crestview, Sam was at the height of his stride in Des Moines. He had even been approached by the Democratic Party to run for congress from the Des Moines district. But he felt he wasn't ready for anything like that.

Judy McClanahan was married to Joe. Their seven-year marriage was a constant storm of separations and near divorce. Sam counseled Judy regularly, trying to help preserve their marriage. Joe, on the other hand, was not religious and wanted nothing to do with religious counseling. He was a six-foot, three-inch, burly truck driver who was more interested in football and drinking beer.

It was a late afternoon in May when Judy McClanahan arrived unexpectedly at the church. The office was officially closed for the day even though Rev. Gashler was still in his study. Judy was at the end of her rope emotionally and felt she needed to talk to the pastor.

Sam heard someone walking down the hallway headed for his study. He got up out of his desk chair and walked to the door. Right away he was met by a tearful Judy McClanahan with mascara running down her cheeks.

"Oh, Pastor, I've gotta talk to you. My marriage is over. I've kicked Joe out of the house. Pastor, I'm through being the obedient little housewife, waiting for her husband while he drives all over the country."

"Sit down, Judy. Let's talk it out."

"I don't want to talk it out! I just want out! Pastor—uh—Sam, I've always admired you as a great man—and a loving husband and father. You have qualities I wish Joe had."

"Thank you, Judy."

"You're so welcome. I really mean it. I've admired you for a long time."

Sam could feel his face turning red, but he secretly enjoyed what she was saying. He had admired her too. She was an attractive woman, living in a difficult marriage. He wished he could ease her suffering and take away her pain.

"Sam, I wish things were different."

"How different, Judy?" Sam asked.

"I mean, I wish we had met first before Joe and Louise."

Sam could feel his heart rate increasing. As she placed her praises upon him, he could feel something building in his heart.

Rev. Sam Gashler was not prepared spiritually or emotionally for what happened that afternoon. He was a man—a supposed man of God—who allowed himself to be seduced by a troubled woman.

Sam and Judy had several clandestine meetings before the guilt and remorse got the best of Rev. Gashler. He decided it had to end before his life and ministry were destroyed. But when he dropped the bombshell on Judy, she didn't take it well. In fact, she became resentful and bitter. She felt alone and betrayed by the man in whom she had placed her love and trust. With the bitterness came threats of exposing the entire affair.

Sam became a tormented man. He often thought, *How could I have been so stupid as to allow myself to get into this mess? If this gets out, my life is over. Louise will never forgive me. The church and everything I've worked for will be destroyed.*

Sam pleaded with Judy by telephone not to expose their affair, but she was determined to hurt him, and hurt him badly—making him pay for rejecting her.

It wasn't easy going about his ministerial duties knowing that, at any moment, his world could explode. Every unscheduled office visit by an elder or church officer almost sent him into a panic. One week went by and then two. Had Judy changed her mind, or would she throw the grenade when he was least expecting it?

Rev. Tony Parks found an envelope slipped under his study door upon arriving at the church one morning. Using a letter opener, he sliced it open and carefully brought the note out into his hands.

It read, "Dear Rev. Parks. You and the Crestview Fellowship Church be aware that your senior pastor and I have been having an affair. I'm writing this note out of concern for my life as well as for the life of the church. A man like Rev. Gashler should not be allowed to continue in the ministry. Sincerely, Judy McClanahan."

Tony Parks held the note for the longest time, trying to examine every word and grasp its implications. The implications outside of Rev. Gashler and Louise would be staggering for the church. In his mind he was asking the question, *What should I do with this? Who would have enough wisdom to help me?*

Rev. Daniel Powers came to mind. He respected Rev. Powers and knew he possessed great wisdom and maturity.

Tony called Rev. Powers immediately to set up an appointment without telling him the subject matter. He would go by the Powers home at one o'clock that afternoon.

"Hey, Tony! Come on in! Mabel, can you get us some coffee, honey? You've got my curiosity up—but I think I know who the subject of our talk is going to be. Rev. Samuel Gashler—right?

"Right, sir. Something has ..."

"Sit down, Tony. Tell me all about it."

"Something has come to my attention, and I need your advice." Rev. Parks was troubled and openly unnerved by what he was about to reveal.

"Go ahead, Tony. What's wrong?"

"Rev. Powers, when I arrived at my office this morning, I found a note slipped under my door. It had been written by Judy McClanahan."

"Oh yes. I baptized her when she was a teenager. What did the note say?"

"Here, you read it."

Rev. Parks quickly unfolded the note from his pocket and handed it to Rev. Powers. Rev. Powers began reading it out loud.

"Oh my, this is a hard thing."

"Rev. Powers, what should I do? What if this note isn't true? I certainly don't want to destroy Rev. Gashler's reputation—especially if it's a lie."

"Well, Tony, I suggest you set up an appointment with

Judy—uh—Mrs. McClanahan and see what she has further to say on this matter."

"What then? I mean, what do I do after that?"

"I'd say, if you feel she's telling the truth, Rev. Gashler needs to be confronted. Tell you what, I'll go with you to see him and we can confront him together."

Rev. Parks breathed a sigh of relief as he shook Rev. Powers's hand. They knelt to pray together before the young pastor was escorted to the door.

A few days went by before Rev. Parks could muster up the courage to call Judy McClanahan. He hated the idea of getting caught up in the scandal and mess this situation could make. He felt trapped in something not of his making but knew he was the only one close enough to see it through.

Rev. Tony Parks dialed the phone in his study reluctantly. His mouth felt like it was filled with cotton, and his heart was pounding so hard in his chest he found it hard to breathe.

"Hello, Judy? This is Tony Parks from Crestview Fellowship. Hi, yes, I got your note, and I need to talk to you about this matter. Would it be possible for you to come to my study here at the church at your convenience? Tomorrow morning? Sure, that would work for me. How about ten a.m.? Okay. Well, I'll be expecting you then. Sure. Okay. Bye."

There was a knock on Rev. Parks's study door at 10 a.m. the next morning.

"Come in, Judy. Please sit down. Can I pour you a cup of java?"

"That would be great. I've been so nervous since you called yesterday. I haven't had much to eat or drink."

Rev. Tony could see she was scared. He admired her courage for stepping out to disclose something so potentially scandalous.

"Do you take anything in your coffee?"

"No, just black."

"Judy, I know this meeting is embarrassing and difficult for you. Why are you doing it?"

"Why am I doing it!" Judy was openly offended by the question.

I'm doing it because Pastor Gashler isn't the man he pretends to be. He's a fake!"

"What do you mean by that, Judy?"

"I mean he comes across to everybody as high and religious and righteous. But he's none of those things. Rev. Parks, I admit I let him into my life. I admit I was lonely and discouraged about my marriage, but he led me into an affair with him. He was so caring and understanding. Before I knew it, we were embracing and kissing, and—"

"Yes, well, you need not give me any details, Judy. All I'm interested in are the facts that he seduced you and that there was an illicit affair."

"Rev. Parks, do you believe me?"

"Judy, how long has this gone on?"

"About four months. But then he stopped calling and didn't want any more to do with me."

"Why did you contact me and not his wife, Louise?"

"Because Louise Gashler is a fine, godly woman. I didn't want her to get hurt."

"Well, if this gets out, she's going to get hurt anyway."

"Pastor Parks, that's why I was hoping you and the church leaders could deal with him, somehow, without hurting Louise."

"I don't know how that can be done or if it should be done. Really, she needs to know about his infidelity without bringing your name into it. I'm not going to share this with our elders—at least not all of them. I'm trying to be discreet about all this. I don't want the church to split or suffer a scandal."

"Pastor, I'm sorry for all of this. Crestview means a lot to me. I'm not attending church now because he's here. When and if he goes, I promise, I'll be back."

"Thank you, Judy, for coming in. I'll be praying for you and this situation. I just hope it can be resolved soon."

"So do I, Pastor. Thank you for listening and understanding."

"God bless you, Judy."

"God bless you, Pastor."

Rev. Parks reported to Rev. Powers his meeting with Judy. It was decided they would have a meeting with Rev. Gashler when he returned home from his speaking engagement.

Sam Gashler returned home to preach the next Sunday morning. On the following Monday, a most rainy and gloomy day, Rev. Parks met Rev. Powers in the church parking lot. Sam Gashler's car was in its usual spot, meaning he was in his study. The two men prayed in Rev. Power's car before entering the church building.

It was 8 a.m., and the church secretary wouldn't arrive until 9 a.m. They would have plenty of time to confront Rev. Gashler before she arrived.

Rev. Parks knocked on Sam's study door.

"Come on in," was Sam's response.

"Hi, Tony. Well hello there, Rev. Powers. How are you gentlemen this rather wet Monday morning? What brings you out?"

Both men were nervous as they approached the two chairs in front of the pastor's desk.

"Please, sit down. What's up?"

Rev. Parks was the first to speak. "Rev. Gashler, the other day, as I was unlocking my study door, I noticed this envelope. It had been slipped under my door. Since it was addressed to me, I opened and read it. Here, I want you to read it."

Sam was puzzled but curious as Tony handed him the note.

"Pastor, we want to know about this. I haven't shared it with anyone in the church except Rev. Powers here."

Shock and fear appeared simultaneously on Sam's face. A long silence filled the room as he read the note and then read it again. Rain was beating down on his study window as he thought of a response.

"Gentlemen, I don't know what to say. Obviously this is a woman who has fantasies about me—fantasies I haven't promoted. I know Judy McClanahan. She's a very troubled woman. I've counseled her. She's trapped in an unhappy marriage."

"You're telling us there's no truth to that note?" Rev. Powers couldn't believe the words of denial he was hearing.

51

"No! I mean, yes! There's nothing to it."

"Pastor Gashler, I met with Judy the other day, and she didn't seem like an emotionally disturbed woman to me. In fact, she seemed more like a woman who was remorseful about getting caught up in an illicit affair with a married man. Pastor, I'm sorry, but I believed her."

Sam's face turned red, and his eyes flashed with anger. "I don't care what you believe, Tony. The fact is I—"

"Whoa! Hold up there with your temper!" said Rev. Powers. "I also believe you had an affair with this woman. I don't think Judy would risk her reputation and life if it hadn't happened."

"Rev. Powers, you've been after me ever since I arrived. You're jealous of my success in building up your dying church. I resent your—"

"Hold up there, son. This conversation isn't about me. I'm irrelevant to what we're discussing here. What's relevant is your relationship with Judy McClanahan. I want you to know that I called her after she had her meeting with Tony. She said she had proof—something about a motel receipt and a manager who remembered you and her together."

Sam's face turned ashen gray.

"Pastor Powers and I take no pleasure in this. We're concerned for the—"

"Oh, yeah, right! Tony, you've wanted my job since my arrival. You were disappointed in the beginning when they brought me to Crestview instead of picking you to be senior pastor."

"Sam, you can say whatever you want about Rev. Powers and me. It doesn't matter. The point is, you are in trouble."

Sam sat back in his chair, looking like a whipped dog. For once it appeared he had nothing to say.

"We're not here, Sam, to destroy you. We're here to help you, as well as to help the church, and Judy too. I'm not here to take your job. I don't want to be senior pastor. I've been satisfied working as an associate. But infidelity in the pastor can destroy this church. Is that what you want?"

"Tony, Rev. Powers, this has gotten out of hand. I certainly did not set out to have an affair. Judy was so vulnerable, and I was so weak."

With that statement, Sam broke down and wept openly, with his head in his hands. His confronters walked behind him, placing their hands on his shoulders.

After several moments of Sam crying uncontrollably, Rev. Powers interrupted by saying, "Sam, you've got to resign. You can't remain the senior pastor of Crestview. You've got to get your life and marriage healed. And you can't do that and be minister of this church."

"What should I do?"

After some thought, Rev. Powers said, "First of all, tell your wife and ask for her forgiveness. Second, write a letter to Judy saying you're sorry, asking for her forgiveness. Don't mail it. Give it to Rev. Parks. He'll see she gets its. And third, write a letter of resignation to the board of elders. They need not know of this matter. Scandal must be avoided at all costs."

"But what shall I say is the reason for my resignation? I mean, they're going to want an explanation."

"Tell them in the letter, as well as to all who ask, that you have some personal problems you need to address. Then drop it."

"What about Judy? Will she keep quiet?"

"Rev. Parks will encourage her to remain quiet. Her husband is no longer a part of her life and knows nothing about the affair."

Samuel Gashler did resign from Crestview Fellowship Church. He also told Louise about the affair with Judy. Her faith in God and her belief that God hated divorce kept her in the marriage. She thought about leaving him for a while afterward but believed it would fuel the rumors about why Sam had resigned his position. Louise spent many hours crying when Sam was not at home. Eventually, she stopped crying and rededicated herself to being the wife and mother God wanted her to be.

# 7

## SIMPSON MEMORIAL CHURCH

Crestview Fellowship Church gave Sam six months' salary. The elders tried talking him into staying as their pastor and taking a six-month sabbatical to work on his personal problem. Instead, a six-month salary was decided upon to help him support his family. The personage was also made available to him until he could relocate. Both Sam and Louise wanted out of Des Moines as soon as possible. A house next door to Sam's mother in Carthage, Missouri, became available, so they moved there, at least, until Sam could find himself.

Sam took three months to recuperate from his emotional wounds. Louise thought it was wonderful having him as a full-time husband and father. He was more attentive and sensitive to her needs and to the needs of their sons. She didn't know what Sam would decide to do with his life. He didn't discuss any of that with her. She really was hoping he would find work in Carthage. She loved her new home and loved her mother-in-law.

One summer day a letter arrived for Sam from Simpson Memorial Church located in Kansas City, Missouri.

"Louise! The search committee at Simpson Memorial Church wants to talk to me about becoming their pastor. Can you beat that!"

"But Sam, it may be too soon for us to consider that. We're happy here. Eric and Allan are doing so well."

"Louise, I'm a pastor. I don't want to do anything else. Yes, I made a mistake back in Des Moines. I've asked God's forgiveness many times since. But I really feel I should at least talk to the people at Simpson Memorial."

"But Sam, Kansas City is such a large city. What about our boys? Carthage has been so good for them. Your mother is good for them."

"Don't you think I know all that? But I've got to go where I feel I can best be used. Kansas City would be a great opportunity for me."

Louise saw that it was no use. Sam had a much stronger will than she did. She backed off to let him do what he must.

Sam traveled to Simpson Memorial Church for an interview. A month and a half went by with no answer from Kansas City. Toward the end of August, Sam received a letter from the search committee telling him they wanted him to preach a sermon at their Sunday morning service the second Sunday of September.

Sam felt this was a good sign—that they were serious about him. He talked Louise into going and taking their sons with them. He wanted to impress the congregation with his beautiful wife and children.

Simpson Memorial Church was impressed with Sam and his family. The congregation voted to call him as their new pastor that same afternoon before the Gashlers left Kansas City. All the way home in the car Sam would talk about nothing else except how wonderful it would be for them at Simpson Memorial and how he planned to build that tired old congregation into a vibrant powerhouse in the metro Kansas City area.

Louise, however, felt nothing but old fears and feelings creeping into her heart. She felt guilty not being able to share in Sam's elation, but she managed to force a smile every time Sam turned to her with another enthusiastic statement.

The Gashlers had one month before their move to Kansas City. Sam's thoughts and actions revolved around Simpson Memorial and his agenda for the church. Louise's thoughts and actions were centered on packing, packing, and more packing. She wanted to enjoy her little cottage in Carthage for as long as she could. She knew life would be changing radically the minute they landed in Kansas City. Her thoughts kept returning to the way it had been at Crestview Fellowship Church in Des Moines and how she had almost lost her husband. Had Sam learned his lesson? Would he continue being the good husband and father he had been since their move to Carthage? Louise desperately wanted that. She prayed to God it would remain so.

The Gashlers arrived in Kansas City on a Wednesday afternoon in the middle of October. The church hired a moving company to move them. Louise had seen the parsonage on her first trip to Simpson Memorial. It was a large, two-story, older home that possessed a lot of character. She was looking forward to giving it the Gashler charm.

Sam landed on the run in Kansas City. He had plans for Simpson Memorial—plans to make this old church into the pride of his denomination. He had done it in Des Moines. He could do it in Kansas City. Sam was grateful word of the scandal had not spread to Simpson Memorial. Things would be different.

Life settled into a routine with the usual sermons to prepare, Bible studies to lead, and visitations to make. Sam didn't have an associate or much staff at all. In fact, his staff consisted of Mrs. Ruth Everly, who worked twenty hours a week as his office secretary.

Simpson Memorial, at its peak in the early 1950s, had been a church of six hundred people. But with the decline of the neighborhood, and with families moving to the suburbs, the church declined to around 150 by the time of Sam's arrival.

The church had declared to Sam their intentions to grow. That was the topic of discussion when Sam was being considered. Sam was soon to find out that what churches say they want and what they actually want can be two different things. Sam found out during his first six months that several of his top older leaders were not willing to make the necessary changes to see growth happen.

Ray Morse was the leader of those objecting to change. He was an elder who projected a great deal of influence into the community as well as into the church. His money was important to Simpson Memorial Church. When Ray spoke, many people listened. He had been a successful businessman, making his fortune in oil. At seventy, Ray was tall, handsome, and distinguished looking. He demonstrated self-confidence and always came across as a man who knew what he was talking about.

Sam entered into an adversarial relationship with Ray almost from the very beginning. Louise thought it was because they were too much alike to get along. Sam thought it was because Ray was a bull-headed know-it-all who always had to have his way. Whatever, their relationship was a disaster waiting to happen.

Sam grew frustrated dealing with people whose minds centered on the past—a past when their church was thriving. He wanted them to see beyond yesterday and see the possibilities of today. He wanted them to envision the future and make plans for it.

He pushed hard for a fleet of three vans to run throughout the city picking up children for Sunday school and church. Ray Morse had it defeated. They weren't needed. Ray didn't want a bunch of little savages running the halls destroying church property.

Sam saw the need for a daycare. He saw a number of working mothers living around the church who desperately needed quality daycare for their children. A great battle erupted at a church board meeting over Sam's proposal. Ray Morse heard about it and had busied himself contacting and influencing certain board members to vote against it. Sam was determined too. He also made several calls, making sure his people were present at that meeting. The daycare proposal won by one vote—although it wasn't clear if anyone really won. Harsh words had been spoken, and nerves had been set on edge.

On the other hand, Sam felt victorious but was oblivious to the fact that Ray Morse was not used to losing—that he was not a man to be crossed. All Sam could see was success. He didn't understand the dynamics of Simpson Memorial Church, nor did he understand the unwritten rules of the games being played there.

Six months had passed since their arrival at Simpson Memorial Church. Louise enjoyed her new home, but she didn't enjoy how she felt around some of the women in the church. She tried to fit in, but there seemed to be some kind of a wall she couldn't break through. For one thing, Eric and Allan were typical little boys, doing what little boys do. She heard grumbling from some of the older ladies that she needed to be firmer with her boys. One lady went so far as to tell her she wasn't a good mother. Louise found herself isolated and lonely. If only she could have a best friend relationship with another lady in the church. It never happened for her the entire time they were at Simpson Memorial.

In spite of Ray Morse's obstructionism, Simpson Memorial was adding new members, but Sam wasn't satisfied with that or anything else happening in the church. After a year at Simpson Memorial Church, Sam felt stymied and frustrated. He was a thirty-three-year-old pastor with dreams and visions for himself and for his church. There were too many obstacles at Simpson Memorial with too many older people standing in his way to success. Not only was he frustrated with his entire situation, Sam was also angry. He openly entered into a confrontational relationship with some of his leaders—especially his older leaders.

Sam's attitude was leading him into the malaise of a power struggle. He wasn't about to give in to the power and money people.

He felt his greatest asset was his ability to challenge his congregation from the pulpit. He decided he would do most of his confronting through his preaching and would begin with a series of sermons on stewardship.

Even though there were several wealthy people in the church, stewardship at Simpson Memorial had been declining for years. Those with money appeared to be more interested in using their wealth to control the church than they were in letting go of some of it to make it viable and growing. Sam decided to address stewardship, or the lack thereof, in a series of three sermons to the end of September when most people would be home from their summer vacations.

Louise was uneasy as she walked into the sanctuary with Eric and Allan. Sam had shared with her some of the thoughts he was going to preach. Old, fearful feelings were creeping back into her heart from their days at Oak Grove Community Church. She remembered the power struggle Sam had entered into with Elvyra Tabias Smythe. Louise was afraid the same thing was going to happen at Simpson Memorial Church. Her father was in the ministry for many years but did not experience the troubles she and Sam had encountered. Her days growing up in parsonages were peaceful and pleasant.

She asked herself, "Why can't we have it as wonderfully as I remember my life being as a minister's daughter?"

Trouble was coming, and she felt helpless. Louise voiced her opinions and fears to Sam, but he didn't seem to share her concerns. Sam appeared cocky and self-confident—not unlike the way he had been at Oak Grove.

Why couldn't they have stayed in Carthage? Life was so wonderful there. Sam was loving and attentive to her and the boys. Why was he obsessed with being a pastor? Louise ached in her heart to live a normal life—free of controversy and stress. She felt another horrible trouble was coming that would drive them out of their established home into uncertainty.

There were people in the church Sam had stroked and courted. It was important to him to have a base of support. Most of these people were under fifty and were not the money people of the church. Knowingly or unknowingly, he was developing an "us against them" mentality among his supporters. An unhealthy atmosphere was spreading. Board meetings were always controversial, and Sunday services were becoming less and less worshipful because of the stress.

Sam looked at Ray Morse as the center of his problems in the church. If only the people could see what Mr. Morse was doing to the church. If only the people would join him in his crusade of bringing change and growth to Simpson Memorial. If only something would happen to take Ray Morse out of his role as patriarch of the church, and destroy the log jam at Simpson Memorial. Then Sam would be able to put things in order. But there was no time to wait for that, at least in Sam's mind. He had to press on for change, regardless of the cost.

Rev. Samuel Gashler entered his pulpit that first Sunday morning ready to launch his verbal assault on the stewardship failings of Simpson Memorial. Louise had thoughts of faking some kind of illness so she wouldn't have to expose herself or her boys to the religious carnage she felt would be coming. But there she was—the faithful minister's wife—sitting in her pew, three rows from the front on the south side of the church where previous minister's wives had sat.

Following his pastoral prayer, Sam opened his message by stating, "Simpson Memorial Church has been a great church. I place my emphasis on 'has been.' It's in decline now, not because it has to be, but because there are some in this church who are not good stewards of that which God has given to them."

There was an immediate tenseness in the audience. A person could have heard a pin drop between Sam's phrases and sentences. Invigorated, Sam pressed on.

"I hear a lot of negative things being said concerning what we can't do. I hear little about what we can do. This church doesn't have a money problem. It has an obstructionist problem. During the last few years the giving in this church has declined. Why is that? Is it because the money isn't there to be given? I think not! Yes, we've seen a gradual decline in membership over the past fifteen years, which has affected giving. But some of you are giving the same amount you gave twenty and thirty years ago. Don't you realize the cost of living keeps going up? So does the cost of running a church.

"This church was great when it had a free flow of visionary ideas. It was great because the pastor and the people possessed a common purpose. But now, so many of you are afraid of growth and do not want it. Others are unwilling to let go of the money to see this church move ahead and prosper once again.

"Over the past ten years, you have had good men in this pulpit—men who left for similar reasons. What were those reasons? I think most of you know. They became frustrated with the few who run this church. These are people standing against everything the pastors proposed. I know this feeling of frustration. I, too, face it.

"Those pastors left because there was also a lack of respect for the minister. The prevailing attitude was and is, 'If the pastor proposes it, it must be suspect.' I don't understand nor do I appreciate that kind of thinking. It's a wrong kind of thinking and must be changed if this church is to be great once again.

"My message this morning is a strong reprimand, but I also want it to be a challenge—a challenge to come away from obstructionism and schism—a challenge to come together in unity for the growth and good of our church. I also want to challenge us all, myself included, to upgrade our giving to a new level so that we can pursue a new day of spiritual and material prosperity here at Simpson Memorial. Let us build together! Amen!"

Having finished his message, Sam nodded to the song leader to lead the closing hymn. He stepped down from the platform and walked down the center aisle to take his place in the narthex.

It had been a rather short but direct sermon. Louise and the boys remained down front in the sanctuary while the people filed out. Normally, she would take her place beside Sam as he greeted people, but she didn't feel like it that Sunday. Sam would have to face the music without her by his side.

Surprisingly, there were no bad comments made about his sermon that day. In fact, there were several words of congratulations. Ray Morse and his wife, Eve, hurried out a side door along with several others. That didn't bother Sam because they never went through the reception line anyway.

The Gashlers received several telephone calls from supporters at the parsonage Sunday afternoon and evening. Sam was bolstered by those calls. Louise wished she could share his optimism. She

61

felt Sam had done a good job of writing and delivering his sermon. She was proud of him and told him so. But down in her heart of hearts, she was fearful of his course of action. Something was going to happen—but what and when?

Sam anticipated confrontation with his detractors all week following his first sermon on stewardship. But nothing happened. Not a peep. He thought, for sure, Ray Morse would pay him a visit. Not only did Ray Morse not pay him a visit, but Ray and his wife decided to leave on a three-week vacation to the Bahamas. Sam saw that as a slap in the face. It was obvious Mr. Morse was sending a message that he did not intend to expose himself to anymore preaching on stewardship. It was also obvious he hadn't received the message well and didn't want anything to do with change or challenges.

The second sermon in Sam's series was delivered to a congregation missing somewhere around thirty of its older members. Sam was not only frustrated; he was angry. The anger was building day by day.

Louise could hardly stand living with him after the second sermon. The anger seemed to be turning into bitterness. He was snappy and critical of everything. She hated to see him coming home.

The third stewardship sermon was not well written, nor was it well delivered. Sam was hurt when he saw that the worship attendance was down by another thirty people. Even a few of his supporters didn't show up for his third message. Sam felt defeated and depressed. Thoughts of resignation came into his mind. Sunday afternoon found him quiet and unresponsive to Louise, Eric, or Allan. They all tried to cheer him up, but it became obvious to Louise that Sam was too engrossed in feeling his sorrow and nursing his bitterness to receive anything from his family. They gave up and stopped trying.

Church life got back to normal after the stewardship series. Church attendance was where it had been, and the Morses came home from their trip to the Bahamas. But nothing had changed.

The church leadership simply decided to ignore Sam, without confrontation or distress on their part. After all, it was their church—not his. They would merely dig in and wait for a legitimate reason to get rid of him.

A two-thirds majority vote of the congregation would be needed to fire Sam. They knew they didn't have those numbers. It would take a real foul-up on his part, or something similar to turn the people against him. The waiting game was on.

Sam decided not to press anymore of his ideas for a while. He had learned his lesson. Instead, he would go about building a larger base of support among the congregation. Not only would he court the younger families, but he would also court some of the older people. Another thing Sam decided to do was preach flowery and entertaining sermons. He would do a little fence mending with Ray Morse. Sam knew they would never be friends, but perhaps they could work together.

On the second anniversary of Sam's ministry at Simpson Memorial Church, it seemed like things were going smoother for Sam and his congregation. He was drawing more support from within the congregation, and all of the people he had brought into the church adored him. The people of Simpson Memorial were feeling good about their church. Still, Ray Morse looked upon Sam Gashler as an adversary who was not to be trusted.

Sam and Louise's marriage had slipped a cog or two. Louise felt Sam was not interested in her anymore. The only passion he demonstrated was for the church. She mentioned her feelings to him, and he even promised to do better. He was more attentive for a while, but then he would get busy with his ministry once again.

Louise was lonely and isolated. A job would have been a good thing, but Sam didn't want her working. He felt she needed to be home for the boys and to do what preachers' wives do. Outside of the Christian Women's League meetings once a month, there wasn't a great deal required of her.

Sam was never there for Allan. Louise would tell him of programs and sporting activities Allan was in, but there was always an important meeting or church conference to attend. She could see hurt and resentment building in Allan's heart. It wasn't difficult for her to relate because she nursed some of those same feelings.

Ray and Eve Morse had a grandnephew who had graduated from seminary and was looking for a position as a youth minister. The church had grown to the place where a youth pastor was needed and could be afforded. In fact, Sam had been researching the resumes and qualifications of several recent seminary graduates. The Morse relative was not one of them.

Most board meetings were routine, and Sam was anticipating nothing different. But he didn't realize what Ray Morse was going to propose that night. It would be a sideswipe of major proportions.

Board meetings were always held in the fellowship hall at Simpson Memorial Church. Everyone seemed happy and cordial as they took their seats in folding chairs facing a long table where the chairman, the treasurer, the board secretary, and the parliamentarian all sat. Dr. Frances Jones, the chairman of the board, always liked promptness. It was 7:00 p.m., and he called the meeting to order even as stragglers were still driving into the church parking lot.

The usual business was completed, including minutes of the previous meeting, the treasurer's report, and various committee reports. Everything was routine until new business.

Ray Morse stood to say, "Mr. Chairman, with all of the new families we've been seeing joining our church, it's obvious to me that we need a youth pastor here at Simpson Memorial."

Sam was shocked and elated by Ray's observation. He wanted to propose a new youth pastor himself at a later date when he had all of his ducks in a row. To hear Ray Morse, the obstructionist, proposing it thrilled Sam to no end.

"Mr. Chairman, I have a grandnephew by the name of Ted Morse who recently graduated from seminary looking for a position, either as an associate or as a youth pastor. Teddy—uh—Rev. Morse could really work out well here at Simpson Memorial. He's not married and wouldn't need much of a salary in the beginning. Mr.

Chairman, I'd like to propose we look into calling Rev. Ted Morse as our new youth pastor. In fact, I'd like to chair a committee to see if he'd meet our needs and qualifications."

Sam was stunned and could feel blood running to his face. The thought of having a Morse on staff at his church gave him instant concern. He could see the potential for tremendous power struggles with Ray Morse in the middle or worse, Ray Morse running the youth program through his grandnephew. He could imagine Teddy answering only to Uncle Ray instead of answering to him as senior pastor. He didn't want any part of it and was ready to nip it in the bud.

"Dr. Jones—Mr. Chairman."

"Yes, Rev. Gashler. The chair recognizes Rev. Gashler."

"Mr. Chairman, I also see the need for a youth pastor here at Simpson Memorial. In fact, I've been doing some research myself. There are several good men available right now in our denomination. But I think it's premature for us to bring up a specific name right now, especially the name of a person related to someone in our church. A great deal more research should be made before calling a youth pastor. Let's look at our options. Perhaps we could—"

"Mr. Chairman, can I have the floor?"

"Go ahead. The chair recognizes Ray Morse."

"Pastor Gashler, my grandnephew would make a great youth pastor. I've been talking to several of the substantial givers in our church, and they're willing to increase their giving to make up his salary, without putting a burden on our budget. I've already spoken to Ted about coming and—"

"You've what! How could you do that! How could you do that without consulting with me as pastor or with this board!"

"Rev. Gashler, don't raise your voice to me like that! I won't put up with it!"

"Ray—Brother Morse, I'm just reacting to your disregard for me as senior pastor. I really should have been consulted on this matter."

"I hardly think so. It's the leaders of this church who make this decision, and I'm one of the leaders of this church."

"Gentlemen, let's get back in order," Dr. Jones said with great apprehension.

Both men were standing on their feet, glaring at one another across the room.

"Now, I think we should cool our tempers and approach this reasonably. Please sit down, Ray—Rev. Gashler. As board chairman I think we'd better refer this matter to a committee. Let's call it a youth pastor committee and let them investigate this matter. We already have a Christian education committee established. How about our calling the people of that committee to be on the youth pastor committee?"

Sam sat down to listen to Dr. Jones's proposal. He felt it had possibilities due to the fact that seven of the eight people on the Christian education committee were young adults with children and teens in the youth program. The down side was the fact that Ray Morse's wife, Eve, was also on the committee. But he felt he could live with that.

Ray Morse also sat down at Dr. Jones's pleading. He was elated at the proposal because his wife was a member of that committee. He could keep tabs on everything through her.

The proposal was moved and seconded. It passed. Dr. Jones quickly finished the agenda and adjourned the meeting. It just happened Sam and Ray got to the side door leading into the parking lot at the same time. Each man offered a weak smile and a tentative nod as they exited the building.

Things settled down for a few days at Simpson Memorial. The Christian education committee was notified about the board's decision. The committee chairperson was Esther Freedman, a mother of a ten-year-old boy and a fifteen-year-old girl. Sam was pleased that she was the committee head. Esther would be open-minded and fair.

As pastor, Sam would be a non-voting member of the committee. The only power he would have was the power to persuade. He felt he had a shot at steering the youth pastor committee in the right direction and away from hiring Ray Morse's grandnephew.

Word came to Sam from Esther Freedman that the youth pastor committee would be meeting the following Thursday evening. He spent the next couple of days before the meeting compiling facts, figures, and possible candidates for the youth pastor position. The fact that some of the wealthier people in the church offered to increase their giving if Rev. Ted Morse was called really bothered Sam. He didn't know how much it would influence the committee's decision.

The youth pastor committee met in one of the senior high classrooms. Everyone was present, including Rev. Sam Gashler. Esther called on Sam to offer the opening prayer.

"We have been given a very important task here," Esther said in opening the meeting. "We want the right man in this position. We don't want to jump at the first candidate without thoroughly checking his credentials. One name has already been suggested. Let's see, his name is—uh—Rev. Ted Morse. I wasn't at the last board meeting, but I believe he is a relative of Ray Morse. Is that right, Eve?"

"That's right. Ray and I wholeheartedly recommend Ted to be our new youth pastor."

"Thanks, Eve. Pastor Gashler, I've heard that you have some reservations about that?"

"Yes, I do!" Sam was trying to stay calm and cool, but he felt his pulse rising with the thought of Ray Morse's grandnephew becoming a part of his staff. "First of all, I believe I should have an important say in who becomes youth pastor. He will be on my staff and under my leadership. It will be important for us to get along, be compatible, and share the same vision. Just because Rev. Morse is available doesn't mean he's the right man.

"Second, he's Ray Morse's grandnephew. How much control will Ray have over his grandnephew? I mean, will he answer to me as the senior pastor, or will he answer to Ray Morse? I believe church staff should answer to the senior pastor. I'm just afraid Ray will have his hands in everything surrounding our youth program. It has the potential for disaster. At least we need to examine our options."

Eve Morse sat quietly without emotion until Sam was finished. "Rev. Gashler, it's hard for me to sit here listening to you questioning the integrity of my husband before this committee. Anything and everything Ray has done is for the good of Simpson Memorial Church. My husband is a good man. I resent what you said about his meddling and interfering in the youth ministry. I just wish that—"

"Mrs. Morse, I've been here long enough to know how things work around here. Your husband is a powerful man in the community and in our church. I've seen him work his way in several programs here at Simpson Memorial. Not many things get done around here without Ray's approval. I can see where that will happen in our youth program."

"Rev. Gashler, you don't even know Teddy. Don't you think we at least ought to have you meet him along with this committee? I don't think it's fair to cross him off the list simply because of your prejudices and insecurities."

The word *insecurities* struck Sam like a bolt of lightning.

"Insecurities! How dare you say that to me! Madam, your husband is a controller. He has to command, control, and manipulate! If I have insecurities, it's because your husband has tried to control or stop everything I have proposed here at this church."

Esther Freedman could see the discussion had become personal. "Pastor—Eve, please! Let's not polarize the business of this committee. Well, committee, don't you think we need to at least have Rev. Morse come to visit with us?"

Everyone agreed except Sam. He merely bowed his head and held his tongue. Round one was lost.

"Eve, will you contact Rev. Morse and see if he will be able to come meet with us on Thursday evening, two weeks from tonight?"

"Yes, Madam Chairman. I certainly will. Thank you for considering Ted."

Sam went home that night with one thought. If Rev. Ted Morse was forced on him as youth pastor, he would quickly resign as senior pastor. No way could he put up with Ray Morse's interference and control through his grandnephew.

Another thought crossed Sam's mind. He wondered if he could influence the parents of the children in the church, along with other people on "his side," to rise up and oppose any move toward hiring Ted Morse.

The next several days found Sam in the homes of most of the families with children and youth. He did his best to plant doubts as to the wisdom of hiring Ray's grandnephew. Most of the young families were fairly new to Simpson Memorial and were not aware of the political strife in the church. Sam did his best to fill them in. A few had picked up bits and pieces of the problems in the church. Some had formed adverse feelings against Ray Morse. Many hadn't.

Then Sam met with certain dissidents in the church who felt as he did. He knew it was important to have his ducks in a row before the next committee meeting.

Sam wasn't looking forward to the scheduled youth pastor committee meeting. He knew it would be a difficult time. It appeared to him the deck was stacking against him. Ray's influence over the committee would be felt through his wife, Eve.

The evening of the committee came. Everyone was present, along with Rev. Ted Morse. Rev. Morse was a tall, gangly young man wearing blue jeans and a Polo shirt. Right away, Sam knew he didn't like him. He wasn't dressed right. Sam felt he should come to an interview in a suit and tie. He'd seen some youth pastors fresh out of seminary before. Some of them tried looking and acting like the kids. Sam believed a youth pastor should act his age and look his age to get the respect of the youth. He didn't like the length of his hair either. It was way too long. He knew he couldn't have any part of working with this young man.

Esther Freedman brought the meeting to order at 7:00 p.m.

sharp. Sam was asked to open the meeting with prayer, as he was always asked to do at all meetings of the church.

"Eve Morse, would you introduce our guest tonight?" Esther asked pleasantly.

"It would be my privilege. I would like to introduce our grandnephew, and possibly the new youth pastor here at Simpson Memorial Church. He's a young man with unblemished character and integrity—a man who studied hard to become a minister and a man Ray and I helped through school. It's my privilege to introduce Rev. Ted Morse."

She introduced him with such enthusiasm that the committee broke out into instant applause. Even Sam caught himself putting his hands together for a couple of beats.

Rev. Ted Morse stood to his feet and acknowledged the committee by nodding to everyone—everyone except Rev. Sam Gashler. It was obvious to Sam he had been warned and well-schooled concerning his description and attitude. Sam felt instant tension coming from the young man standing in front of him.

Esther Freedman asked Rev. Morse to give them a rundown of his educational credentials. Then she asked him to share with the committee his vision for a youth ministry at Simpson Memorial.

"Well, Mrs. Freedman, if I become youth pastor I will do my best to organize the youth into weekly youth meetings. I will also organize a monthly activity, such as bowling, roller skating, and other special activities. We could have fundraisers such as a car wash and a chili supper to raise money for a once-a-year youth trip—such as going to Colorado skiing. I've given it a lot of thought and prayer. I believe youth need to be taught the Christian life through word and example. It can't be all activities and little gospel. I believe in a balance between the two."

"Thank you, Rev. Morse. Your answers were truly inspiring."

It was obvious Esther Freedman was sold. Eve Morse was beaming with pride. The rest of the committee displayed facial expressions of pleasure as well. Sam felt things were sliding against his wishes. He even thought Rev. Morse's speech was impressive, but Sam couldn't get beyond his being a grandnephew to Ray Morse. He knew it just wouldn't work with Ray waiting in the wings to control and manipulate.

Esther invited questions from members of the committee, purposefully leaving Sam for last.

"Okay, thank you all for your questions, and thank you, Rev. Morse, for your honest and candid answers. Now, I'd like to ask Rev. Gashler to ask any questions he may have.

"Esther, I only have one question. Rev. Morse, you have impressive credentials and a tremendous vision for youth ministry. I find no fault with any of that, but you are a grandnephew of one of the most influential men in our church. What would you do if your uncle attempted to pressure you into doing what he wanted? You see, Ted, I'm the senior pastor here. I believe the youth pastor should be subordinate to me and not to an uncle. Do you see what I'm getting at?"

"Rev. Gashler, I respect you as a minister and as the spiritual leader of this church. You would be my minister. But I respect my granduncle too. Yes, he is an influential man. And yes, he does express strong ideas about certain things. I'm not going to dismiss everything he says just because he's my granduncle. I'm not going to do everything he says just because he's my uncle. I think it all can be worked out. I see no problem—"

"Well, I do, Rev. Morse! I've had run-ins with your uncle before. He's a strong and powerful personality. I don't think you could buck him if there was a challenge to him."

"I can't sit here and allow my husband's good name be slandered by you, Rev. Gashler. You should be ashamed of yourself. Ray is a godly man and has sacrificed a lot for Simpson Memorial."

"Eve—Rev. Gashler, please don't do this." Esther Freedman was determined not to allow the meeting to disintegrate any further. "I think we've heard enough from Rev. Morse and Rev. Gashler to form a recommendation to the general board. I invite the two ministers to leave now so that this committee can talk openly and then vote."

Although the senior pastor sat in on all committees and boards at Simpson Memorial as an ex officio member, he was not to sit in on this discussion and vote. Rev. Ted and Rev. Sam left the meeting and the building while the youth pastor committee carried on with their business.

Later on that evening the phone rang at the parsonage. Sam answered.

"Rev. Gashler? This is Esther Freedman. Pastor, our committee voted to recommend Rev. Morse to the general board to be our new youth pastor. I realize this is not what you wanted, but the vote was unanimous except for one abstention. Eve Morse felt she shouldn't vote because he is her grandnephew. I thought you'd want to know as soon as possible."

"Thanks, Esther. I appreciate your call. Goodnight."

Sam wasn't surprised by the decision. He knew the vote would go against his wishes. His last line of defense would be the families with children and youth, as well as those who felt the way they did about Ray Morse.

The next general board meeting was scheduled for the following Tuesday evening. It would be a crossroads for him and the church. A fight was coming as well as an important vote. His ministry at Simpson Memorial stood in the balance.

The night of the board meeting was rainy and cold. There were many more church officers and congregants at the meeting than usual. Tension filled the air.

Rev. Ted Morse sat with Ray and Eve Morse. Rev. Sam Gashler sat with Louise. For the number of people gathering in the fellowship hall, the crowd was relatively quiet.

Dr. Frances Jones, chairman of the board, called the meeting to order at exactly 7:00 p.m. by asking Rev. Sam Gashler to open in prayer.

"Thanks, Pastor, for that fine prayer."

Dr. Jones took the meeting quickly through most of the agenda down to Old Business. "Under old business we have a report from the youth pastor committee. I call upon Esther Freedman for that report."

Esther was obviously nervous about what was going to happen. The paper in her hand was shaking uncontrollably.

"Mr. Chairman, our committee met last Thursday with Pastors Gashler and Morse present. We asked Rev. Morse to give us a rundown on his educational credentials. They are impressive. Then we asked him to give us a vision for youth ministry here at Simpson Memorial—which he did. He was inspiring. After giving each member on the committee a chance to ask questions, I gave Rev. Gashler a chance to do the same. After asking his questions, Rev. Gashler voiced some concerns, which this committee took under advisement. The two pastors then left our meeting so we could be free to discuss and vote. Bottom line, Mr. Chairman, our committee voted unanimously, except for one abstention, to recommend to this board that Rev. Ted Morse be called as our youth pastor. That's my report and our recommendation."

There were some unsolicited comments and sighs of disapproval expressed by several people in the crowd.

"Ladies and gentlemen, let's keep our comments under control, to be expressed in the discussion time! Thank you for that fine report. Esther, my thanks and appreciation to the entire committee."

Applause broke out from those in the crowd who agreed with the recommendation.

"Rev. Morse, you've been recommended to this board for the position of youth pastor. Before I open the meeting up for discussion and vote, I would like to call upon you to express your thoughts and feelings about your ministry here at our church."

"Thank you, Mr. Chairman, for the opportunity. First of all, I'd like to thank the youth pastor committee for their recommendation. I'm humbled. As I told the committee, I'd like to organize our children and youth into weekly youth group meetings. I'd like to see monthly fun activities, such as bowling and roller skating. I mentioned to the committee that we could have fundraisers such as chili suppers and car washes to raise money for once-a-year youth trips. Youth ministry is my specialty and passion. That's what I studied to become. Thank you all for your consideration."

The room was quiet. Many were impressed openly by the young man. Sam knew it would be an uphill battle.

Even Louise was impressed with the presentation she heard. She knew, however, that she could never express her feelings to Sam. It was a moot point since she wasn't a member of the board and had no vote.

"Rev. Morse, I'm going to ask you to leave the meeting now so that we may openly discuss this issue and bring it to a vote. Thank you for coming to our meeting tonight."

The young man nervously smiled at his aunt and uncle as he left fellowship hall.

"Rev. Gashler, as our senior pastor, I want you to come forward and express your thoughts on this issue."

As Sam made his way to the front, it was obvious by the crowd noise that many were anxious about where the meeting might go.

"Thank you, Mr. Chairman. I've been your senior pastor for six years now. In that time, I have come to understand the needs of our church and the problems we face. As senior pastor it is my responsibility to see and express the direction we should take as a church—to this board and to the congregation.

"I have nothing personally against Rev. Morse. He's a fine young man, and he will make some congregation a wonderful youth pastor. I just feel that, under the circumstances, it wouldn't work for him to be here at Simpson Memorial.

"I believe the senior pastor should shape and guide the church staff, including the youth pastor. Rev. Morse has family in the leadership of our church. To me, that spells conflict of interest. Who would he listen to? Who would he answer to—to me or to his family?

"Mr. Chairman, I see problems ahead if we pursue this. I see a schism coming in our church if this particular man is hired. As the general board, I encourage you not to call this man as youth pastor. There are other people qualified to take this position. Let's shop around for a while and not be hasty here. I have a list of five possible candidates myself. Let's give this some time. That's all I have to say on this matter."

"Thank you, Rev. Gashler. I'm opening the meeting up for comments from the floor."

"Mr. Chairman."

"The Chair recognizes June Forrester."

"Thank you. I think Rev. Gashler is afraid he might lose some control in our church. If we hire Rev. Morse, it seems to me he—uh—Rev. Gashler, would not be able to control him. It's a matter of power and control with the pastor. I really feel . . ."

"Now wait just a minute here, June!"

Sam couldn't hold himself back. His face was turning red. Louise looked startled but wasn't surprised by his outburst. "It's not me who wants total control and power of this church. It's Ray Morse. I'm trying to keep us on track here. Ray is the one who is pushing this thing through. Personally, I'm offended by and tired of his controlling spirit. Everything has to go his way, or nothing goes at all. No one person in the church should have that kind of power."

"Except you?" Mrs. Forrester shot back.

"June, I'm not looking for power and control. I'm looking for success. This has the word *stifle* written all over it. Ray Morse wants to stifle the church programs wherever he can."

Ray Morse couldn't hold it in any longer. "Mr. Chairman, I've heard enough of this. I'm not going to sit here and be insulted and slandered by this—this hireling. I've studied our good reverend here, and I see a man who is more interested in pushing his own career than he is in caring for this flock. He's trying to build a monument to himself out of Simpson Memorial Church. I'm not the only one who has noticed that. There are other leaders who have recognized this trend. Rev. Gashler needs to humble himself and take a good, long hard look at his motives. That's all I've got to say in response to his personal attacks."

The others in the room remained quiet during the verbal battle.

"It's unfortunate that this discussion has become so personal and poisonous." Dr. Jones was obviously disgusted by what he heard.

"Rev. Gashler—Mr. Morse, you both need to reconcile your differences so that this church can go on in peace. You both have people on your side. There is a split among people in our church over the hiring of Rev. Morse as our youth pastor. It could get out of hand here. I encourage all of you to go ahead and vote your consciences, but respect the outcome as God's will. Please don't hold grudges or cause problems in our church if the vote doesn't go your way.

"Before we take a vote, are there others wishing to join the discussion? But please keep your words away from personal attack."

The discussion continued for another forty-five minutes. Both sides of the issue spoke candidly and honestly about their feelings. Three people became so upset they had to leave the meeting before the vote.

"Ladies and gentlemen, it's time to take a vote. A paper ballot is being distributed to you. Only members of this board are eligible to vote. Write yes if you're in favor of our calling Rev. Morse. Write no if you're against it."

A simple majority of the vote would be needed to call Rev. Morse. Sam didn't like the odds. He wished the church by-laws required two-thirds vote. The odds would have been more in his favor and against Ray Morse and his crowd.

The ballots were counted. The vote was 59 percent in favor of calling Rev. Morse. Ray and Eve Morse broke out into applause along with their supporters, while those who voted against it moaned and groaned. Some didn't do anything at the announcement.

Dr. Jones brought the meeting to a reasonable adjournment.

Tension settled into the congregation following the controversial board meeting. The words that had been spoken between Ray Morse and Rev. Sam Gashler spread like wildfire. A schism had come to the surface. It was causing suspicion among the church leaders. People who had been friends for years were no longer speaking to one another. Even some families were split over the issue.

Blindness settled over Sam's heart. All he could see was his dislike for Ray Morse. He wouldn't call it hatred, but Louise knew it was. She had to live with it. It was eating him up inside.

Sam started getting chest pains. His doctor told him he needed rest and less stress in his life. But Rev. Sam Gashler was a workaholic. He lived to work—to build. Ray Morse, he felt, stood in his way to making Simpson Memorial a great church.

Ray Morse, on the other hand, wasn't stressed at all. Rev. Ted Morse was now the youth pastor. All was well except for the fact that Rev. Gashler was still senior pastor.

He had defeated Rev. Gashler. It was a sweet victory, but he was about to launch a crusade to remove the unsuspecting pastor from his position.

Ray Morse received a call, one day, from an anonymous woman living in Des Moines, Iowa. She informed him of Rev. Gashler's problems at Crestview Fellowship Church. He was given the whole story of Sam's infidelity. Ray asked her how she knew of these things. Her only response was that she was close to the woman Sam had had the affair with.

What should he do with this information? If it was true, he could use it to get rid of Rev. Gashler. If not, he could be liable. After speaking about it with three of his closest friends in leadership, Ray decided to have a little talk with the good reverend.

After being announced by Sam's secretary, Ray was ushered into his study.

"Good morning, Ray. How are you this morning? Please, sit down."

"Pastor, I'm going to cut to the chase. I've received word that you had an illicit affair with a woman at your church in Des Moines, Iowa. Is that true, or is it not?"

Sam's face instantly grew beet red. He hated the man sitting across the desk from him. He was shocked—to the point of emotional and physical duress. Sam didn't know how to respond. Pain became a part of each heartbeat. His mind was swimming, and his heart was seemingly about to pound its way out of his chest.

Ray knew he had scored a direct hit on the pastor.

"Get out! Get out of my office!"

"You haven't answered my question. Did you have an illicit affair in Des Moines, Iowa?"

All of a sudden, Sam was out from behind his desk with his hand on Ray Morse's left arm, pulling him violently toward the door of his study. He literally pulled and then shoved Ray from his office.

Ray Morse was enjoying every second of Sam's overreaction. It gave him more ammunition to rid Simpson Memorial of the hireling.

"Reverend, I know who and what you are. Better get your things packed. Your ministry here is going to come to an abrupt conclusion. Either you resign or we're going to call a short meeting of the church board. Get your hands off of me!"

Ray left the church that morning exhilarated. He smelled blood and victory. *It won't be long now*, he thought.

Sam was so upset he had to go home. He could feel despair overtaking his mind—despair like he had never felt before.

Louise was puzzled when he arrived home at 9:30 in the morning. It was totally out of character for him. He wouldn't answer any of her questions and went straight to bed.

She knew something had happened at the office, but what? Louise called the office secretary, Jessica Hammond, to see if she had any answers.

"Louise, there was a big blow-up between Rev. Sam and Ray Morse. I couldn't hear all they were saying, but I know your husband threw Ray out of his study."

Louise knew at that moment it was over. Sam had crossed the line. There would be no return.

Sam was devastated. His despair grew deeper. But Louise couldn't get anything out of her husband. All he wanted to do was sleep. In fact, he had Louise call the board chairman, Dr. Jones, to ask for two weeks off. He got it, but it wasn't a pleasant or restful time for Louise. Sam slept most of the time and became more demanding of her as the days dragged on. Louise was beginning to entertain old thoughts—thoughts of leaving Sam. She, too, was at the breaking point.

One afternoon toward the end of the two weeks, Louise entered their bedroom and sat on the bed beside Sam.

"Sam, you've got to snap out of this! I can't go on. Our boys can't go on. You're making our lives miserable.

"I don't know what happened between you and Ray Morse, but you've got to get out of this bedroom and get on with your life. We love you and are depending on you."

"Louise, I have nothing more to give—to the church or to you."

"Well, then, Sam, does that mean it's over between us?"

"No Louise, I—I—I ..."

"It's going to be if you don't come around. I'm not going to stay here to watch you destroy yourself. You're a much stronger man than this. I believe you can get up and get on your way. You can fight whatever it is that has brought you down."

"Louise, I love you! Please don't leave me. I need you and the boys."

"Then get up out of this bed and face whatever it is you must face! You can do it. I know you can!"

Rev. Sam Gashler did get up out of his bed of despair to face his problem. But the only way he knew to resolve the problem was to resign. He couldn't afford a scandal. It would have ended his career.

# 8

# FRANKLIN FELLOWSHIP CHURCH

The Simpson Memorial Church didn't heal much after Sam's resignation. His supporters felt betrayed by his resignation. They couldn't understand why he resigned so abruptly. After all, they were ready to stand by Sam in opposition to Ray Morse and his bunch. But Sam knew he couldn't tell them the real reason why he quit.

The forces of Ray Morse were in control of the church after Sam left. Ray had won, but a good one-third of the people left Simpson Memorial when they saw it was no use bucking the firm grip of power that had taken over the church.

Ray Morse and the church board gave the Gashlers one month to vacate the parsonage even though Sam wanted two months to find a new church. Furthermore, the board decided that he be suspended of all duties of the church immediately with pay.

Sam was bitter. Louise could see that. She noticed that his ability to bounce back was damaged. He looked older than his forty years.

When several of the people came to him for advice concerning what had happened at Simpson Memorial, he flat out told them to leave the church. And leave they did. A few of the people were so fed up with church politics they never went to church—any church—ever again.

The word got out through denominational channels that Rev. Samuel Gashler was available, but he received only one call. Franklin Fellowship Church was a small church of one hundred people located in a rural area of northwest Iowa.

Sam was desperate to move because his month in Kansas City was running out. It didn't take much thought or consideration. He had little choice. His district superintendent recommended he take it—that it was a fine small church. The rural setting would be good for him and his family.

Louise was excited about their move to Franklin Fellowship Church. She would have a good-sized garden again, and country life promised a slower pace. She hated the city. The parsonage at the Franklin Fellowship Church was only five years old. Only one pastor's family had occupied the large ranch-style house, which sat across the road from the church on two acres of land.

The Franklin Fellowship congregation was fairly wealthy, with several successful farmers in the church. She had been told they would never have to buy milk, meat, or produce again—that the farmers were extremely generous to their pastor's family.

Sam wasn't as excited about Franklin Fellowship Church as Louise was. He was glad to be moving away from Kansas City to Franklin Fellowship Church but wasn't looking forward to the isolation of a country church in northwest Iowa. The closest city was Sioux City, but it was seventy-five miles away.

Louise and the boys thrived in their new home. Sam, on the other hand, merely took it from day to day. Outside of an occasional hospital call, he didn't have much to do. He felt unchallenged and unfulfilled.

Louise knew he was having trouble adjusting, but she chose to ignore it. She wasn't going to allow Sam's problems to affect her joy, peace, and happiness. The people at Franklin Fellowship were friendly and loving. Louise hoped Sam would learn to love and appreciate them—that he would eventually settle in and be happy too.

Sam did settle in to a semi-mood of contentment. He continued to feel stifled, but he liked having less stress in his life.

The congregation fell in love with Louise and the boys. She was extremely busy with women's ministry and missions. At all of the other places they had been, she lived in the shadow of her husband. At Franklin Fellowship Church she was asked to take an important part in the various programs. Louise thrived and grew during her time there.

The Gashler marriage was doing much better too. Eric and Allan, as well, had a full-time daddy. There was peace in the house—a peace like there had never been before. Louise felt God had opened the door for them to move to Franklin Fellowship Church so that they could become a true family.

Louise hoped, though she never shared it with Sam, that they would be able to raise their boys at Franklin Fellowship Church and live the rest of their lives there. Life never had been so good, and she wanted it to go on forever.

Sam, on the other hand, didn't have quite the contentment he saw in Louise. He wanted it, but there was something deep inside of him that wanted more. But he didn't want to disturb Louise's serenity. She had suffered much during their years together. He felt she and their sons deserved a haven like Franklin Fellowship Church.

The church was conservative and evangelical. Sam knew that when he accepted the call. He determined from the beginning he would not share any of his liberal views on abortion, divorce, war, and human sexuality with his congregation. He concentrated his preaching and teaching on more traditional aspects of the Christian faith.

Sam was asked, one time at a denominational pastor's retreat, what he truly believed. He shared many of his liberal views with several other pastors in the discussion group. Surprised, one of the more conservative pastors asked, "Do you feed any of that to your people?"

"Oh no!" Sam replied. "If I did that, they would immediately be searching for a new pastor."

"Well, then, what do you preach and teach at Franklin Fellowship Church?"

"I give them Bible stories with life applications, but I stay away from doctrine and social issues. I preach feel-good messages. They eat it up."

It was obvious by the expression on the other pastor's face that he was disgusted by what Sam had shared.

It was a cold but sunny day seven months into their ministry at Franklin Fellowship Church when Louise went to the mailbox positioned at the side of the road in front of the parsonage. She was looking for the usual bills and a possible letter or two from her family. What she found among the other letters gave her instant anxiety. It was an envelope marked Emmanuel United Church of Davenport, Iowa. She had heard the congregation was looking for a new pastor. She also knew it was a church rebounding from a split over the previous pastor.

Her first thought was to dispose of the letter as quickly as possible. Then her Christianity kicked in and she knew it would be wrong to do that. She would have to give it to Sam unopened.

Sam arrived home after visiting a parishioner in a Sioux City hospital that afternoon and walked in the backdoor of the parsonage.

"Hi, honey! How was your day?"

Louise didn't know how to answer that question. It had been a fine day until she went to the mailbox. "Fine. Go get washed up and call the boys in for supper. It's almost ready."

Sam took notice that something was bothering Louise, but he knew she would eventually tell him what was on her mind.

Nothing was said about the letter during supper—just the normal chitchat. It wasn't until Sam said good night to the boys that Louise took the opportunity to give him the unopened letter.

"Sam, a letter came in the mail for you today. It's from the church in Davenport, Iowa. I didn't open it because—because—well ..."

"A letter? Why didn't you give it to me when I first got home?"

"Because I was a little upset and didn't want to go through supper with a big discussion—especially in front of the boys."

"Louise, you're something else. This letter may not be anything. Getting yourself all worked up won't help anyway."

"I know, but ..."

Sam used the penknife he always carried with him to open the envelope. He carefully unfolded the letter and read it to himself.

"Honey, what does it say?"

"Well, they want to talk to me about being their pastor."

"Sam, no!"

There was a panic in Louise's voice. She knew that was what the letter was all about. She knew she should have destroyed it before Sam got home.

"Louise, all they want to do is talk to me. Don't get upset, honey."

"Sam, I know how you are. I realize you feel stifled here at Franklin Fellowship Church. Even though you haven't said much, I can sense your restlessness. But things have been going so well for us. We have a beautiful home and a loving church. Life here has been wonderful for our sons. You can't seriously consider taking them out of this environment. Don't do this to them—to us! Think of your family for once in your life."

Louise broke into tears. Sam tried to comfort her by putting his arm around her shoulders, but she obviously possessed some stored-up feelings. The dam broke and the emotions flowed out freely.

Nothing was said about the letter for a few days. Sam placed it on his desk at the church and often read it to himself. He really wanted to talk to the search committee in Davenport. He felt he was drying up inside being at a church as isolated as Franklin Fellowship. He needed the growth potential of a city church—the excitement of seeing things bust loose.

Louise lived in anxiety. She didn't know what was going on in Sam's mind. She knew instinctively what was in his heart. But she didn't know what plans he was making, or what plans he wished he could make.

One morning the phone rang in Sam's office.

"Reverend Gashler? This is Brian North. I'm the chairman of the search committee here at Immanuel United Church in Davenport."

"Oh, yes. I received your letter a couple of weeks ago. Sorry I haven't answered it."

"That's okay, but I just wanted to touch base with you to see what your thoughts are. Would you be interested?"

"Yes, Mr. North, I'm interested, but there are some things I've got to work through and take care of before I can seriously talk to you about moving."

"Reverend, we have plenty of time. Our church called an interim minister to pastor here until a new pastor can be called. So there's no hurry. I must tell you that you are on the top of our list of potential pastors. We know of your talents and gifts. I personally heard you preach a dynamic message at our denominational conference in Chicago several years ago. It was tremendous."

Sam was immediately stimulated by the comments of the young man on the other end of the line. He craved and thrived on the appreciation. It was as if someone had opened the window to let in a fresh breeze for his soul.

"Thanks, Brian, for the encouragement. Tell you what, I'll take a couple of months to get some things settled, and then I'll be free to sit down with you and your committee. Is that acceptable?"

"Rev. Gashler, I think that would be fine. Go ahead and do what you have to do. I'll give you another call in sixty days to see if you're ready to talk to us. But if you get things settled before then, please feel free to give me a call or write me a letter."

Rev. Sam Gashler was stimulated and excited after the phone call, but he knew he had to work gently with Louise. That wouldn't be an easy task.

Sam didn't say anything to Louise about the phone call from Brian North. He knew it would upset her. There was no need to do that until he had definitely made up his mind.

Louise instinctively knew something was up. She felt Sam's mind and heart were no longer with the Franklin Fellowship Church. In ways she sensed he had become distant from her. He was on edge and more apt to explode when things didn't go right. He was also spending less time with her and the boys. She even mentioned her concern to him, but he just brushed it off as part of her paranoia.

The opportunity in Davenport, Iowa, was never far from his thoughts. Sam had even written for literature about the city from the local chamber of commerce. It concerned Louise when she noticed it on the top of Sam's desk one Sunday morning. She wanted to ask Sam about it but knew it would only cause trouble between them.

Louise learned to be a silent sufferer. She endured much and knew when it was best to keep her mouth shut. It was difficult butting heads with the Rev. Samuel Gashler. He always was confident, at least on the outside, and knew what he wanted and where he wanted to go. Down deep inside Louise knew Sam's mind was made up concerning the church in Davenport. She knew, no matter how loudly she protested, he would win out.

The inevitable came on a Tuesday evening seven weeks after Sam's conversation with Brian North. The boys were in bed, and Sam was anxious to get the matter of moving to Davenport settled one way or the other. Sam ushered his reluctant wife into the living room.

"Honey, we've got to talk about—"

"About what?" As if Louise didn't have a clue.

"We've got to talk about Immanuel United Church—about our moving to Davenport."

Sam could see the distress on Louise's face. He sensed her displeasure in having to discuss anything he was about to bring up. But he had to. He couldn't go another day or another hour without getting it settled.

"Louise, you know how I feel even though we haven't talked much about it. I must tell you that I received a call from the search committee chairman shortly after we got his letter. That was seven weeks ago. I told him then I would think about it and try to work some things out. I told him I needed two months—then I'd get back to him."

"Sam, I feel you've shut me out. In my heart I knew you were seriously thinking about Davenport. I felt you were afraid to discuss it with me. I'm hurt that it took all this time for you to talk to me about it—for us to work it out."

"Well, I knew how you felt about Davenport—about Franklin Fellowship Church—about our life here. I knew you were upset with their letter. That's why I didn't say anything to you about the phone call from their search committee chairman. I was afraid..."

"Afraid of what? Afraid of me? Sam, I'm your wife! I'm committed to following you wherever you go. I may not like it, but I'm committed."

"Honey, will you follow me to Davenport?"

There was a pause as Louise thought about the importance of her next few words. "Yes, I'll follow you to Davenport. Do I want to leave here? No! Do I think it's a good move for you—for me and the boys? I don't know. I just don't know! Do I trust your judgment? Honestly? I'm apprehensive about that. There's something in you, Sam, that pushes you to try to be the biggest and the best. Frankly, that scares me. In the past it has led us into power struggles and heartaches. In Des Moines it almost destroyed our marriage. I don't think I could take it if it ever happened again."

At that moment Louise broke out into tears. Sam instantly embraced her, putting her small frame into his arms.

"Oh, Louise, I love you so very much. It hurts me to see you cry. I promise you, I'll never be unfaithful to you again. I'll never—"

"Sam, there are different kinds of unfaithfulness. Sometimes I think I could handle another woman better than your huge appetite to succeed in the ministry. It takes you away from the boys—from me.:

Tears were welling up in her eyes again and began to pour down her face. Sam once again pulled her close.

"Honey, I promise you that—"

"Don't promise me anything! I've heard you promise things before. I won't have you play those games with me again. No promises! All I want is your love for me and our sons. All I want is to know we're at the top of your priority list. Not the church. Not your travels, or your ministry. I want God first in our lives and then our marriage and family. Understand me?"

Sam thought he understood. "Yes, I understand."

"Good. I have a suggestion. Let's pray about this tonight, and let's pray for the next week about it. If you still feel the same way next Tuesday night, then we'll go—in spite of my anxieties."

With that said, Louise offered her hand. The two of them sat on the couch, lowered their heads, and prayed. Sam's prayer was formal and preacherly. Louise's prayer was honest, warm, and childlike.

# 9

# IMMANUEL UNITED CHURCH

B rian North was very gracious, and the Immanuel Church was
most generous in helping the Gashlers move. Money was no
object. It was obvious the church wanted Sam Gashler as their
new minister. Louise felt good about their wanting her husband to
be their minister. At the same time she was anxious because Sam
might take that as a blank check to run wild in pastoral ambition
and mold the church to his design. She had seen that before—with
disastrous results. But things were going well, and Sam was happy.
Wasn't that what counted?

Immanuel's church building was huge, with a seating capacity
of a thousand. Its glory days had been in the 1940s and 1950s. It
was still a good-sized church, at eight hundred in attendance for
Sunday morning worship.

Sam was careful not to say much to Louise about his ambitions.
He really wanted to build the church back to its days of glory and
influence. And he thought Immanuel was a city church that had
had several of the denomination's more liberal pastors over the
last thirty years. He wouldn't have to suppress his words to fit a
conservative audience. He would be free to preach anything he
wanted.

As the pastor of one of the larger Protestant churches in town,
Sam had access to several organizational points of power in the

community. He loved the notoriety and respect. He felt like he was back on track. But he felt like he was, at times, walking a tight rope between his life in the ministry and his life with Louise. Her words still echoed through his mind.

Immanuel United Church was known for being the church of politicians, doctors, attorneys, and businessmen. He lacked for nothing. His salary was more than exceptional. His office was fabulous, with its own private bathroom complete with a shower. He had a staff of three associate ministers and one Christian education director, along with an executive assistant and three secretaries. The most unusual staff person was his executive assistant, Gladys Troop.

Gladys was a jewel. She was always at the beck and call of the pastor and his staff. It was Gladys who ran the office and oversaw the three secretaries on staff. It was obvious Gladys loved life. As a forty-five-year-old divorced woman with three grown children, she had experienced some difficult times. Yet, she was always bubbly, energetic, and helpful.

Sam wanted to do well in his relationships with the other pastors on staff. At forty, he was the oldest man on staff—which was good because of this title of senior pastor. It was even printed in gold on his office door.

Louise liked the palatial parsonage—as she called it. She felt like a queen. There was even a cleaning lady hired by the church to take care of the house. It took a while for Louise to get used to another woman being in charge of the house. It had always been her responsibility to take care of their home. But not as long as Jessica (Jesse) Watson was on the job would Louise ever have to mop, dust, or do any other household chores.

Part of the package with the Gashlers moving to Davenport was Louise's involvement in all of the women's activities in the church and community—which were several. She had enjoyed working with the women at Franklin Fellowship Church. Her role there had been less rigorous and more supportive. At Immanuel she felt pushed to lead and excel. Her life had radically changed, and she was overwhelmed, at times, with the growing challenges.

The three pastors under Sam's leadership had different ministries. Guy Post was the minister of evangelism. Robert Henderson was the minister of pastoral care. Bill Lyons was the minister of music. And then there was Sondra Pierson, who was non-clergy but who was in charge of the Christian Education Department.

Sondra hadn't been out of college very long. She was single, attractive, and extremely knowledgeable of her field. She was competent and wanted everyone to know it.

Bill Lyons was a different story. Bill was talented and arrogant. He performed his duties well—with a great deal of flair. But Sam knew Bill was not a team player. He believed Bill was out to promote and do what was best for Bill.

Louise thought privately that the reason Sam and Bill were at odds from time to time was due to the fact they were so much alike—strong-willed, arrogant, and self-serving. Of course, she would never have shared her thoughts about that with Sam.

It was obvious Sam was the senior pastor everyone wanted. He was intelligent, sophisticated, energetic, and reasonably liberal.

Immanuel United Church was a social church. They desired sprinklings of the Bible, but not enough to stifle their lifestyles. No sermons on holiness were wanted. No sermons on commitment to Christ and no sermons against drinking or gambling would be heard from the pulpit at Immanuel. That suited Rev. Gashler just fine. He wanted to fit in with their lifestyles.

# 10

## Problems at Home

Eric had graduated from high school four years before and was in the University of Iowa. It had always been his passion to become a doctor. He wasn't sure what his specialty would be, but he knew he wanted to help people.

Allan, on the other hand, was in his last two years of high school. Rev. Gashler looked upon his second son as a real challenge. It seemed Allan resented his father and didn't want much to do with the church. His interest was directed more at doing as little as possible at school and home. No matter how much his parents pushed or threatened, Allan wouldn't respond. They even took him to a psychologist at one point, without much success. In fact, Dr. Freedman told them there was not much he could do without their son's cooperation.

Allan did have an interest in cars—not just any cars, but hot and fast cars. His father thought his interest was a waste of time and tried to channel his thoughts toward more academic pursuits, like geometry or one of the languages. Sam knew his son was a good baseball player and tried to encourage Allan to join the high school baseball team. But Allan was not interested. The more his father insisted, the more Allan resisted.

Eventually it was impossible for Louise and Sam to get Allan in Sunday school or church. That happened on Sunday morning in the winter of Allan's senior year.

One Sunday morning Louise knocked on Allan's door to wake him up. "Allan, it's time to get up and get ready for Sunday school. It's seven thirty and we've got to be at church by nine."

Louise assumed he had heard the knock and call to get up. The pastor was already at the church, as was his custom, by 7:00 a.m.

When it got to be 8:15, Louise became concerned about their being late.

*Where is that boy?* she thought to herself as she climbed the stairs to his bedroom.

She knocked and entered Allan's room, only to find him still in bed.

"Allan, aren't you feeling well? Honey, it's time to be up and ready for Sunday school and church."

Allan began to stir until his elbow was pushing his head and shoulders up from the pillow.

"Mom, I've made a decision. I know you and Dad are not going to like it. Mom, I'm not interested in the church or religion in general. You go ahead to Sunday school. I'll be all right."

Louise was stunned, yet she had known something was happening within her son.

For a few minutes Louise tried to talk him into at least going to worship. But Allan wouldn't budge, turned over, and pulled the covers over his head. With that, Louise left the room.

*What will Sam think or do when I tell him about Allan's defiance?* she wondered.

Louise went ahead, finished getting ready, and walked the few steps next door to the church building. All through Sunday school and church she worried about her son—about what Sam would do when she told him of Allan's decision. Her heart ached inside her chest.

Pastor Gashler did not notice the absence of his son in the church service. He was into his sermon too much to notice Allan's absence. Sam was enjoying the exhilaration of the people's compliments about how wonderful his message and delivery had been.

Louise stood by her husband as the people filed out of the sanctuary. She dreaded having to tell him about Allan. *Not before or during lunch,* she decided. Sam always took a nap after Sunday lunch. Perhaps she would break the news following his time of rest.

Meanwhile, Allan was gone when they got home after church. At first, Sam didn't realize Allan wasn't home. But then he began to wonder and inquire of Louise, "Where's Allan?"

The words swelled up in her throat as she tried to speak.

"Well, where's Allan?" he asked again.

"I don't know where he is. I haven't seen him since I left the house for Sunday school this morning."

"Didn't you get him up this morning?"

"Yes, I woke him up, but he told me he didn't want to go to Sunday school or church—that he wasn't interested anymore."

Shock and then anger came across the face of Rev. Samuel Gashler. "Louise, where is he now?"

"I don't know. I checked his room, and he's not there."

Different thoughts flooded Sam's mind as he sat down at the kitchen table—Louise dutifully preparing lunch.

*What are the elders going to think? What are the people in the congregation going to think? How can I minister or counsel my people if my own son won't come to church and is rebelling?* All of those thoughts raced back and forth across his mind.

"Honey, it's time for lunch."

Sam immediately came to from his thoughts, realizing there was a sandwich with potato salad sitting in front of him.

Around 8:30 that evening, Allan came into the house through the kitchen door. At first neither Sam nor Louise were aware of his presence until they heard him opening and closing cabinet doors, looking for the peanut butter.

Both parents entered the kitchen—Louise in a docile mood, Sam in a hostile and angry mood.

"Allan, I want to talk to you!"

"Dad, I know what you're going to say, and I know you're hurt and angry."

"Sam rushed Allan, knocking him up against a kitchen wall, causing a clock to become dislodged, crashing to the floor.

Louise was horrified. "Sam! Stop! Don't hurt him!"

Allan had a shocked and scared look on his face. His father had never, ever been physical with either son before. Both father and son looked deep into each other's eyes, seemingly, to Louise, for an eternity. Sam still pressed his arms against Allan's chest when the front door bell rang.

The thought of someone at the door broke the intensity of the moment. Louise rushed to answer the door.

As Sam and Allan rushed into the living room to see who was there, a tall police officer came into view.

"Sorry to bother you folks, but I'm here to question your son, Allan."

"What is this all about, Officer? What has he done?" were the rapid-fire questions coming from Rev. Gashler's mouth.

"Sir, Rev. Gashler, I'm not sure he has done anything. I only know that two hopped-up cars were drag-racing on the edge of town. One was a yellow Camaro, and the other was a red Mustang. Son, I see a yellow Camaro in your driveway. Does it belong to you?"

Sam spoke up before Allan had a chance to say anything. "Officer, did you see the race happen?"

"No, Reverend. It was reported by a witness to our department. We haven't found the red car, but we're pretty sure the yellow Camaro in your drive was involved."

Sam knew Allan was the one who raced the yellow Camaro, and he knew the officer must talk to his son about it. "Come on in, Officer. Please sit down. Allan, you sit here across from the officer—Officer Jenkins, isn't it?"

"That's right."

He was familiar with the Gashlers. His wife and children attended Sunday school and worship at Immanuel United Church.

"Allan, I'm not here to arrest you. I'm here to give you warning not to do anything like that again. It's dangerous, and you or someone else might get hurt or killed. Do you understand me?"

Allan understood, all right, and acknowledged what Officer Jenkins had said without saying or promising too much.

On the other hand, Sam said, "Officer, I'm going to make sure he'll not do anything like that again!"

The police officer excused himself and left the three Gashlers to themselves.

Louise retired to the sanctity of the bedroom, knowing Sam and Allan were not finished. She only hoped Sam would calm down to a gentler state of mind.

.    "I can take your keys away from you. Is that what you want? Huh, is that what you want?"

"No, Dad, I don't."

"Allan, I'm disappointed in you. It's not just the drag-racing. It's your rejection of the church and ultimately of all that I stand for."

"All that you stand for? Dad, what do you stand for? Do you stand for us as a family? Dad, you're gone most of the time to some meeting or conference. Even when you're home, you seem far away. If that's what church and religion means, I'm sorry, I'm not interested."

Sam felt, at that moment, that there would be no use in continuing the conversation. Personally and religiously, he had lost his son. He said no more and left the room with a heavy heart. Neither he nor Louise would get much sleep that night.

# 11

# THE COMING STORM

Rev. Samuel Gashler and Louise tried to show the church and community their lives were perfect—no problems and no tension in their marriage or home. Several of the church leaders asked Sam about Allan's absence from Sunday school and church.

One of the leaders was Allan's Sunday school teacher, Don Appleton. He was alarmed after Allan's third week being absent.

"Pastor, I've noticed Allan isn't coming to my high school Sunday school class. I've also looked for him in worship. Is anything wrong? Can I be of help?"

Just the thought of someone approaching him about this flaw in his perfect family made Sam cringe. What could he say to Don's question?

The question was asked following church one Sunday. Sam saw an opportunity to be rushed in answering the question.

"Don, it's complicated. Allan is just going through a phase. But thanks for asking."

With that, Sam took Louise by the hand and left the building.

Life for Sam was normal, at least in his every day schedule. He was a hard worker, expecting the same from his staff at the church. It became obvious to his subordinates that something was wrong. Word had gotten out that Allan was not being seen at church. Some of his Sunday school classmates had seen him chumming with a low-life named Paul "Chic" Sommers. The Christian education director, Sondra Pierson, received the word from one of her youth.

Sondra did not like Rev. Gashler very much. She had been criticized on several occasions. Sam told her she needed to dress more appropriately for her position. Casual was her style. Sondra wanted to wear blue jeans and tennis shoes. That was unacceptable to Sam. He wanted her to wear a dress, or at least, slacks and regular shoes. She conformed, but their relationship was strained afterward.

Not content to remain quiet about Allan, Sondra told each of the staff, including the office secretaries. It was obvious she wanted to get back at the senior pastor. After all, wasn't it her duty to tell the others what she had heard?

Bill Lyons had also received some criticism. His ministry was to select the music for worship, lead the choir, choose the instruments, and occasionally, sing a solo. Rev. Gashler, he felt, was always interfering with his choice of music—especially the style of music he chose. The senior pastor wanted more of a traditional style. Pastor Lyons wanted contemporary, complete with guitars, drums, and keyboard.

Both men tried to compromise. Both tried a middle ground, but it became obvious there was a growing tension between the two pastors, affecting the rest of the staff.

Sondra Pierson and Bill Lyons would meet for coffee from time to time across town at a local cafe. The topic was always Rev. Samuel Gashler and their dislike of him. It wasn't only his interference they didn't like. They didn't like his style of ministry. It appeared to them everything had to revolve around him. As they put it, "He is the great controller."

They liked their jobs and loved the church. Neither Sondra or Bill wanted to endanger their positions. All they could do at the moment was talk and complain to each other.

After three years at Immanuel United Church, Rev. Gashler was getting restless. It wasn't because things weren't going well.

The church was growing, and he had received notoriety in the community and the denomination. He couldn't get over Allan's rejections. He felt Louise was drifting away from him. It wasn't that he believed divorce was imminent. Louise was raised not to believe in divorce. But he could tell she had withdrawn emotionally from him. Louise seemed tired and unenthusiastic about her duties in the women's ministries as well.

There was another problem raging in his heart and mind. He felt God was far away. His preaching was being affected by his doubts about the virgin birth and the resurrection of Jesus. All of this he knew and had studied throughout his career. It was easier for him to preach on political and social issues than to preach on Christian doctrines or Jesus's birth and resurrection.

Sam knew what Louise believed about His life, death and resurrection. She had been raised in a conservative pastor's home. She believed in Jesus. She believed all of the things she had been taught in Sunday school and church. Her mom and dad taught life's lessons in the home through their Christian examples. Sam understood that but always felt uncomfortable being around them.

He thought, *Do we need a marriage counselor? No! What if it got back to the church we were having marital problems? I'm supposed to have the answers. I'm supposed to help other people and not need help.*

It seemed he was being torn between his professional life and his private life. In his public life he knew how to perform and how to appear confidently in control. But his private life was not what it should be. He did not have any answers for what he was going through. He wouldn't dare go to one of the other pastors on his staff. He must not appear weak to any of them.

Allan had graduated from high school the year before and had gone out on his own. For a while he moved into an apartment with another young man, but they didn't get along, so he moved into a one-room efficiency apartment by himself.

He got a job at a local garage. Allan loved cars. He loved being around his boss, the owner of the garage, John Hodges. John knew what he was doing and had no problem sharing his knowledge with Allan. They developed a real bond as they worked together. John had no trouble telling Allan he felt the youth possessed great potential as a mechanic. His comments bolstered Allan's confidence in himself, and he knew being an automobile mechanic was what he wanted to do with his life.

Pastor Gashler kept track of Allan, although they had little contact. Louise, on the other hand, would frequently stop by his apartment at night when Sam was in a meeting or out of town for a conference. She always brought him chocolate chip cookies or an entire lemon pie, which was his favorite.

The tension in the church office continued. One morning Rev. Guy Post knocked on Sam's door.

"Come in."

"Pastor, do you have a minute?"

"Sure, Guy, please come in and sit down. What's on your mind?"

It was obvious Rev. Post was a little uneasy. He highly respected Rev. Gashler and didn't want to do or say anything to hurt their working relationship. Yet, he knew he had to say something.

"Pastor, I think we work well together. Don't you?"

"Yes, of course." Sam was growing uneasy—picking up on Pastor Post's uneasiness.

"Pastor, there's some kind of a problem here in our office between you and some of the staff. I don't know if you're aware of it or that you can feel it, but I felt I should come to you with it—to see if—"

"Yes, yes, I'm aware of it. I'm aware that Bill and Sondra don't think much of me. They don't like me criticizing them. Bill resents my exerting leadership in the music of our church, and Sondra—well, she simply doesn't like me."

"Why do you think that is?"

"Some of it may be because I've talked to her about dressing better for church and ministry. I realize there is tension among my staff. What about you, and what about Rev. Henderson? How do you feel?"

"How do I feel about the situation, or how do I feel about you?"

Rev. Post was growing more uneasy than before. "Rev. Gashler—uh—Sam, I don't always agree with everything you say in your sermons. To my taste you're pretty liberal in your views. My taste is more biblically oriented. But I'm committed to working with you or whoever the senior pastor is."

"Guy, you are a good man! Thank you for coming to me with your concerns."

"Sam, can we pray together about these problems before I leave?"

"Uh, okay. Do you want to lead?" At that moment Pastor Gashler didn't feel much like uttering a prayer.

Pastor Post prayed a sincere and specific prayer—that Rev. Gashler and the staff would work out their problems. Sam gave a rather distant ecclesiastical prayer that said nothing about the staff problems.

Rev. Post left Sam's office a little bewildered. He didn't know if his conversation with the senior pastor had been helpful or not. Time would tell.

After Rev. Post left, Sam set back in his chair with clasped hands behind his head to mull over the entire conversation.

He thought, *Should I bring all of this to our elder board? What would that do? How would they respond? No, it could cause a schism in the church. After all, the staff members were here when I came. They were well-established before I arrived as senior pastor. No, I must work this out in a staff meeting.*

Pastor Gashler did not realize Pastor Bill Lyons had gone to a couple of church elders concerning the problems between some of the staff and Pastor Gashler. It really wasn't a surprise to most on the elder board. They indirectly had heard rumors over the last few months. There had even been discussion on what should be done. In reality nothing was decided. It was easy to let it slide and hope the situation would improve.

Sam was continuing his spiritual battles. All of his training and all of his experience could not help him in the conflict of soul and spirit. Some days he felt he was going through the motions at work. He knew it would be just a matter of time before people would take notice something was wrong with him.

One afternoon Sam was out making shut-in calls and found himself driving between calls. All of a sudden, he pulled over, shut the engine off, put his head on the steering wheel, and proceeded to cry uncontrollably. The dam had broken, and the tears were flowing down his cheeks in a flood of emotions. It was a good fifteen minutes before he was able to bring his emotions under control—before the tears stopped—before he could dry himself off.

Sam felt better having relieved the emotional stress. He started the car, put it in drive, and drove back to his church office.

Louise prepared Sam's favorite meal of pork steak, hash browns with white gravy, and green beans. She knew it would please him—and it did. During the meal, they talked about some of the activities of the day. Most of it was routine stuff.

Then, all of a sudden, Sam blurted out, "I had a crying fit in the car this afternoon!"

Louise was taken off guard. "What? What do you mean?

"I mean I was driving down the street when I found myself pulling over. I couldn't stop the tears. Louise, I cried like a baby for quite a while. It felt so good when I was finished. I guess the pressure had built up so much it had to be released. So I cried."

"Sam, what's going on? You have always been in control and under control. Now it seems things are different. I've noticed it, and I'm worried about you. I'm worried about us. Even your sermons, at times, appear to be disjointed and rambling. Sam, what's wrong?"

"Honey, things are not going well with some of my church staff. Pastor Bill Lyons and Sondra Pierson do not respect my leadership. I'm constantly in conflict with one or the other of them. They've been doing a lot of griping to other staff members. I'm worried that it's all going to crumble down around me."

Louise believed there was more to it than staff problems, but she didn't know how to approach the issue. She had lost touch with him emotionally over the past few years of their life together. He always had to be in control. She always had to be subordinate to him in some way or another.

"Sam, how's your health? How's your blood pressure?"

"My health is fine. My blood pressure is always a little high, but that's to be expected in my profession. I do take blood pressure pills. They help keep it down—a little bit anyway."

Louise felt his sharing a bit of his emotional life helped him and brought her, for the time being, back into his emotional realm.

It was a total surprise when Sam received a telephone call from Frank DeWitt, chairman of the elder board.

"Pastor, this is Frank DeWitt. How are you today?"

"Hi, Frank. Oh, I can't complain. What's up?"

"Pastor, I've been asked to call a special meeting of the elders along with you and the other members of your pastoral staff. How about tomorrow night—Thursday at seven p.m.?"

"Frank, what's all this about?"

"Something has come to our attention that needs to be settled— hopefully at least."

Sam hated controversy. He knew what was coming. "All right. Where's the meeting being held?"

"In the conference room next door to your office."

"Okay, Frank. I'll see you tomorrow evening at seven p.m."

It seemed like an eternity as Rev. Gashler waited for Thursday night. He didn't sleep much Wednesday night. He couldn't concentrate on sermon preparation. Thursday afternoon he decided to take a long walk in the city park. His thoughts centered on what he would say in response to his critics—mainly Sondra and Bill.

At supper that night Sam shared with Louise his thoughts about the upcoming meeting. She wasn't too surprised but was apprehensive about how her husband would respond. She knew he could get hyper in a hurry. She knew he could become angry to the point of losing control.

"Honey, I'm concerned about your temper. There is already animosity between you and others in your staff. Please don't get angry. You must stay cool and calm."

"Louise, you're absolutely right. I'll try to be godly."

Rev. Gashler was already seated at the conference table with Frank DeWitt when the rest of the elders and pastoral staff arrived. There were ten church elders present.

Sam's stomach was in knots, and his nerves were like a rubber band having been pulled to the max.

Frank DeWitt called the meeting to order and asked Rev. Gashler to give the opening prayer.

"Our great and wonderful heavenly God, we humbly come before You. Be with us in our deliberations tonight. May Your will be done. Amen."

"Thank you, Pastor. As chairman of the elder board, I was asked by several elders and one staff member to call this meeting tonight. A problem has developed among our pastoral staff—a problem that seems to be growing, and the only way I know to resolve the problem is to bring it out in the open tonight. Let's air it out so we can have unity."

"Mr. DeWitt, can I say something?" It was Rev. Bill Lyons holding up his hand.

"Yes. Go ahead and speak."

"I have some concerns, and yes, I have issues with Rev. Gashler. The church hired me to be in charge of the music program. He and I are always at odds on the music. I know he is my boss, but I also know he is controlling and condescending. He is somewhat arrogant and doesn't respect me. I hate it when he talks down to me. Both Sondra and I have issues with Rev. Gashler."

Sondra Pierson was surprised she was being brought into the conversation so soon. But she knew it was time to say her piece.

"I, too, find working under Rev. Gashler's leadership difficult. For some reason, he doesn't like the way I dress. Repeatedly he has criticized me for wearing jeans and T-shirts around the office. I always wear acceptable clothes to the children and teenagers of our church. Their parents haven't complained. Of course, on Sunday mornings I always wear appropriate clothing—usually a dress or blouse and skirt. Also, I'm not sure of his spiritual leadership. He doesn't appear to know or care about us as human beings. As Rev. Lyons has said, he just wants to control us."

Chairman DeWitt turned to Rev. Gashler for his comments.

Sam was seething inside and wanted to tell them off in no uncertain terms. But he remembered the words of Louise: "Stay cool and calm."

"Mr. Chairman, I too am troubled because of the lack of unity among some staff members—mainly with Sondra—Miss Pierson—and Bill Lyons. I know they have conspired together and have shared some of their feelings with other staff members. I've said nothing over the months this has been going on—for the sake of our staff and church."

As Sam shared his feelings, he felt a bubbling of emotions, much like a volcano just before it erupts.

"Personally, I'm appalled at Sondra and Bill's attitudes. They have resented me ever since I became senior pastor. They've talked behind my back. Yes, it's true, I have confronted both of them at times, but it's because my job is to see the church runs smoothly. It's my job to—"

"Wait just one minute!" Sondra interrupted. "What does what I wear to the office have to do with the church running smoothly? I find that insulting and demeaning!"

"Sondra, sometimes you come to the office looking shabby. Your jeans have holes in them."

"Rev. Gashler, that's the style today. I'm only trying to relate to the kids."

Before Sam could respond, Rev. Lyons broke in. "May I say something, Mr. Chairman? Rev. Gashler, you are about forty years behind in your approach to worship music—to Christian music in general. The younger generations use guitars, keyboards, and drums. They like to express themselves through lots of praise music. I thought that was the direction the church wanted to go—especially with the youth in mind. But when you came, all of that changed. That's when this conflict started. I believe it's a matter of which way the elders want Immanuel United Church to go."

Chairman Frank DeWitt interrupted. "I think we need to interject the thoughts and feelings of our other two pastors, Rev. Post and Rev. Henderson. Pastor Post, do you have something to say?"

"I don't know exactly what to say, other than the fact that Rev. Gashler, in my opinion, is a little hard on Sondra. I'm for anything that will reach children and young people for Christ. Sondra has a good heart and wants to influence children and youth for the good. Whether the choice of dress does that or not, I don't know. And as far as the worship goes, I can't say. I'm not musically inclined. Perhaps the two pastors are both right and wrong about their style of music—especially church music. I believe it's a matter of individual taste. That's all I have to say."

Chairman DeWitt then turned his attention to Rev. Bob Henderson. "What about you, Rev. Bob—what are your thoughts?"

"Chairman DeWitt, I like and appreciate every one of these staff people, but something definitely has broken down—communication on a personal level for sure. It's obvious their different approaches and opinions have turned into suspicion, dislike, and hopefully, not hatred. We've got to get beyond what Sondra wears and what music is used in our worship service. I believe the main issue is love, respect, and personal attitudes. If we don't deal with internal spiritual problems, the external will never be resolved. There's got to be repentance, forgiveness, and change of attitudes—change of the heart."

Chairman DeWitt felt the meeting had gone as far as it should. He didn't want it to become a shouting match or worse. Mr. DeWitt felt Rev. Henderson had made some fantastic points.

"Okay, everyone. I'm going to bring this meeting to a close. Next Tuesday evening is our regular elders' meeting, at which time we elders will discuss the issues brought up tonight. This meeting is adjourned."

Sam was troubled by the meeting. He didn't feel good because he hadn't been allowed to say more. His adversaries scored points with the elder board, and he didn't get a chance to rebut their charges.

Sam was disappointed in Guy Post and thought for sure he should have been more on his side. *Oh, what a milquetoast*, he thought.

Rev. Gashler didn't know what to think about Rev. Henderson's presentation. In reality, he was becoming increasingly bothered by it. All of the talk about repentance and forgiveness hit him hard. He thought he was a spiritual man—wasn't he? He was a pastor. He was a well-known spiritual leader in his church, community, and denomination. He had counseled people. Why should he receive counseling from a subordinate such as Rev. Henderson? Why, he was a good fifteen years younger, with a lot less experience.

Sam tried to keep a normal routine schedule leading up to the Tuesday evening elders' meeting. Chairman Frank DeWitt informed him that he was not to be present because the elders needed to talk candidly about the staff problems. He was always a part of the elders' meetings. Being there would have given him some leverage. He could push his agenda a little more. Now they would discuss the problems without his input.

On Tuesday afternoon Sam went home to Louise. He couldn't stand being at the church office and needed some tender loving care only Louise could provide

Louise was in the kitchen as Sam came in the back door. "Sam, what are you doing home?"

"To tell you the truth, I couldn't stand being at the office—so I came home to be with you."

"With me?" Louise asked the question with more of a harsh tone.

"Yes, you!" Sam's tone was much the same.

Louise was puzzled. Sam rarely came home in the middle of the afternoon. "Okay, what's wrong?"

"Nothing's wrong except tonight the elders are meeting without me. I don't know how it will turn out or what decisions they will make."

"Have you prayed about it?"

Louise's question hit Sam as if it were a new concept. "Well, sort of—I mean I did ask God to vindicate me and help the elders decide in my favor."

Louise could see her pastor-husband would be difficult to convince there was much more to prayer than what he had originally prayed for.

Louise was busy preparing a pork roast with carrots and potatoes for the evening meal. Sam seated himself at the kitchen table.

"Hey, can I have your full attention?" he snapped.

"No, because I've got to get the potatoes peeled and cut up for the roast. I'm listening. Go ahead."

"Louise, I'm hurting inside. I'm hurting because my authority as senior pastor is being challenged. I'm hurting because this mess was brought to the elders' board. I'm hurting because—well because, I feel God is somehow punishing me."

"Why would you say that?" she questioned.

"I feel this way because things aren't going the way I planned. I had such high hopes for Immanuel—for my career."

Louise thought about Sam's answer as she busied herself at the sink. She had heard much of the same thoughts about his plans and his career before. In the past she never felt it was her place to say much about his ideas. That was the point. He always talked about his ideas and his plans—his career. She always believed it was her duty to be an obedient pastor's wife, willing to go where Sam wanted to go.

"Sam, you're always talking about your plans—your ideas and your career. Have you just once asked God for His will to be done in your life? After all, it's a part of the Lord's Prayer, isn't it?"

Rev. Samuel Gashler could see he wasn't going to get much sympathy from his wife. It was time to retreat to the living room, where he laid down on the couch to think and possibly, take a nap.

After supper Sam spent the evening watching the University of Iowa basketball team on television. The time went slowly. He was expecting a call from Chairman Frank DeWitt explaining the results of the elders' meeting. But Frank did not call that evening, which caused much distress for the senior pastor. Sam slept little that night.

Sam went to his office as usual the next morning. Around ten a.m., Frank DeWitt knocked on his door.

"Good morning, Pastor. Can I come in for a minute?"

"Sure, come in and sit down."

"Well, we had our meeting last night. We started at seven p.m., but the meeting didn't conclude until after ten thirty. That's why I didn't call you last night. But I needed to inform you this morning."

"Inform me of what?"

"Inform you of what we discussed and what we decided should be done."

"Okay, what's that?" The pastor nervously asked.

"The elders' board recommends to you and to Sondra and Pastor Bill Lyons that you enter a time of repentance and forgiveness, just like Rev. Henderson recommended. We didn't see any other solution—other than firing somebody."

Sam was taken aback by the decision. Repentance and forgiveness were for other people, not for him. He hadn't done anything to repent of. The others were the culprits. It was they who had gotten out of line by questioning his leadership as senior pastor.

The elders' board didn't have any guidelines as to how reconciliation was going to be accomplished between the opposing parties. They had only suggested that it needed to happen. Reconciliation could only take place when and if Rev. Gashler, Rev. Lyons, and Sondra Pierson examined their own hearts to humbly see the need for repentance and forgiveness.

The more Sam thought about the elders' suggestion, the more irritated he became. *They should have stood with me*, he thought. *How can I continue being the senior pastor of the church? How can I have the respect needed to lead Immanuel?*

Within a week of the elders' meeting, Frank DeWitt stopped by Sam's office to check on any progress he may have made.

After knocking, Frank opened the door to peek his head inside. "Hi, Pastor. Can I come in? Are you busy?"

"Come on in, Frank."

"Thanks Pastor. I thought I'd better stop in and see how you're doing. Rev. Lyons and Sondra Pierson have expressed their willingness to meet and pray with you. Rev. Henderson has volunteered to lead the prayers of repentance and forgiveness. What do you think? Are you willing to meet with Bill and Sondra, along with Pastor Bob?"

Sam could feel anger rising within his entire body. His heart was pounding hard within his chest. His eyes looked up from his desk, meeting Frank's eyes in seemingly an eternal stare.

"Frank, I'll be honest with you. No, I'm not interested in going through any of that. It's a personnel problem—not a spiritual one. If anyone needs to repent, it's them."

Frank DeWitt was shocked by Rev. Gashler's answer. How could the man he thought was a great spiritual leader not want reconciliation?

"Rev. Gashler—Sam—that's not the right attitude for you to take. I don't see how you could ever have the respect of the church elders if you don't at least meet with the others for prayer. Rev. Henderson is neutral and will simply lead the prayer meeting. You won't have to confront Bill or Sondra. Just come and see what will take place. It might—just might—be something good."

The response from Rev. Gashler was quick and sharp. "Sorry, I'm not going to go and humble myself before any of those people. They have been insubordinate. They are the ones who have questioned authority—my authority as senior pastor."

"Don't forget, Pastor, you're supposed to be under the authority of the elders. The elders are supposed to give you guidance. There's a checks and balance system involved. You must submit yourself to the elders as spiritual leaders. We can't and won't give you free rein over the affairs of this church. As chairman of the elders, I strongly am telling you to go to the prayer meeting. What have you got to lose?"

"Frank, let me know how the prayer meeting goes. I'll be waiting for their repentance. And I'll certainly forgive them if they ask me to."

Chairman DeWitt could see his conversation with Rev. Gashler wasn't going anywhere. He got up from his chair, excused himself, and left the room.

Sam knew his days as senior pastor were numbered. He sensed that his taking a stand against the elders' board would cause much trouble in the church. He had seen those kinds of church problems in other places he had been.

That evening, after supper, Sam laid out to Louise his morning conversation with Frank Dewitt.

"Louise, I'm not going to be a part of any prayer meeting of reconciliation."

"But Sam, the elders have called it. You can't refuse to go. Don't you realize your position as senior pastor at Immanuel United Church is at stake? Sam, please reconsider!"

Rev. Gashler was hoping for some much-needed sympathy from Louise—that she would see his position and agree with him. But Louise could feel and see beyond the personnel problems and attitudes of Sam, Sondra, and Bill. She understood the spiritual dynamics of repentance, forgiveness, and reconciliation. She had been taught and had seen it as a child growing up in a pastor's home. Her father was a spiritual leader in the true sense of the word. But Sam, she knew, had some real issues he hadn't been willing to deal with over the years she had known him. She knew she could only go so far in their conversation.

Louise loved her husband and felt down deep he could become a tremendous spiritual man—a true man of God. Yet she believed it couldn't be done through her manipulation. Only the Holy Spirit would be able to bring change to his heart and life. Only God could make Sam into a true man of God. That had been her prayer for many years.

The conversation ended with Sam's angry words about his detractors and why the elders should have sided with him. Louise did not say a word after that.

The prayer meeting of reconciliation came and went without Rev. Samuel Gashler's attendance. The report was made from Rev. Henderson to Chairman DeWitt the next day.

Without Sam, the prayer meeting was not too meaningful. Rev. Bill Lyons and Sondra Pierson did express their desires to change their attitudes and seek spiritual healing. But Pastor Henderson was shocked and disappointed that the senior pastor was not there.

For several weeks the atmosphere in the church office was tense. Even the secretaries knew about the troubles among the staff and were affected. Rev. Gashler isolated himself in the confines of his office except when he had to be out making calls or attending community meetings.

Sam was growing more and more despondent and depressed. Louise noticed his moods and was concerned for his mental and physical health.

One afternoon Sam came home, sat down at the kitchen table, placed his elbows on the table, and started weeping uncontrollably as Louise entered the room.

"What's wrong, Sam?" she asked.

"Louise, I can't continue pastoring here in Davenport anymore. It's becoming unbearable in the office. The elder board continues to put pressure on me. I've noticed some of the people in the congregation are now ignoring me—giving me the cold shoulder. How can I pastor a church that is increasingly losing respect for me?"

"Sam, haven't you caused all of this controversy? Haven't you brought all of this on yourself?"

Through his tears Sam could see Louise was not giving him the sympathy he felt he needed. Surely she would understand, of all people. But it was obvious her heart had hardened somewhat against him.

"Louise, I've done nothing wrong, and I will not budge. I will not give them the satisfaction of seeing me cave in to their demands."

She could feel anger coupled with disappointment rising within her being. Finally Louise spoke, letting it all go.

"Sam, I've almost had it! You are egocentric, prideful, self-centered, and spiritually blind! You don't have the good of the church at heart. All you think about is yourself and your ministry!"

The crying stopped, and Sam was drying his eyes and face. "Louise, how can you—"

"And furthermore, I think you ought to resign. The Immanuel Church needs a senior pastor who is not an emotional wreck. It appears you can't lead this church any longer. Your staff is unable to follow your leadership, and I don't think you have the ability to lead them or the congregation."

Rev. Gashler appeared hurt by what Louise had said, yet down deep inside, he knew she was right.

A few more days passed before Sam truly realized he must submit his resignation to the elder board. It did not come as a surprise to them. In fact, they were secretly hoping he would since he refused to meet their demands—or as they originally said, "their suggestions."

Some in the congregation were shocked and disappointed when they heard. Others were relieved, believing things would settle down and church life would get back to normal.

# 12

## FIRST CHURCH OF SANDUSKY

Sam and Louise moved to Dubuque to be close to her aging parents. Both were in ill health. Some of the Gashlers' furniture was stored, and the rest was used in their two-bedroom apartment three blocks from her parents' home.

Louise secured a position as a clerk at a dress boutique. Sam had some difficulty finding a job. He kept hearing employers telling him he was overqualified. But eventually he was hired as an administrator at a local nursing home.

For three years the Gashlers lived a normal life in Dubuque, Iowa. Louise loved being close to her mom and dad. Within a year of each other, her parents died. First her father died and then her mother. Louise was devastated. She was close to both her mom and dad. As time went on, her life got back to normal, but normal for both Louise and Sam would soon change again.

Sam always subscribed to the denominational periodical *The Beacon of Faith*. Within every monthly issue there were always listings in the back of churches from all over the country looking for ministers. One day a church listing caught Sam's attention. It read, "Church of 200 congregants needing an experienced minister in Sandusky, Ohio. First Church of Sandusky."

He hadn't given up the idea of pastoring again. Being a nursing home administrator was a decent job, but pastoring a church was in his blood. Sam loved being up front. He craved the admiration and notoriety of being a pastor. He enjoyed being called "Reverend."

Then his thoughts went to Louise. How would she feel about his pastoring again?

The Davenport experience had almost done her in—had almost done him in as well.

The Rev. Samuel Gashler had to throw his hat into the ring and see if Sandusky would contact him.

A few weeks later, Sam received an answer to his letter. The pulpit committee was interested in talking to him. Would he travel to Sandusky for an interview?

He knew he would have to talk to Louise about the possibility of moving to Sandusky. What would she say? How would she react?

It was Friday night, their "date" night. They always went to a nice restaurant and sometimes, a movie. This night they decided to relax, talk, and enjoy a fairly expensive meal. All the while he was thinking of how he would introduce Sandusky, Ohio, into the conversation. After the salad and before the main course, Sam spoke up to express his thoughts.

"Louise, I've been contacted by a church in Sandusky, Ohio, to be their pastor. They want to visit with me."

Before Sam could utter another word, Louise said, "Oh, Sam. Not another church! How could you even consider pastoring again? Didn't Immanuel Church break your desire to ever pastor again? You almost had a nervous breakdown in Davenport."

"I know all of that, Louise."

"Aren't you happy being a nursing home administrator? It's a good-paying job with great benefits. I really like my job at the dress boutique. I'd really like to stay here in Dubuque."

Sam felt troubled, yet he knew there would be opposition from Louise. He knew she would not want to move anywhere ever again. Could she be persuaded? Could he somehow change her mind?

For several days Sam and Louise said little to each other. Sandusky did not come up in any communication between them at all. Sam wanted to bring it up on several occasions but didn't. He feared a bad reaction from her.

What Sam didn't realize was, Louise was thinking and praying about the move. She could feel her husband's disappointment over her not wanting to be a pastor's wife again. She loved Sam and knew he wasn't satisfied with his job in Dubuque. It hurt her to see him not feeling fulfilled. He didn't say anything about it, but she could sense it. She also sensed that it was putting a barrier between them. Sam didn't have to put up an argument or say anything about it. She knew. The pressure was always present. They needed to talk.

It was evening. They had finished supper. Louise knew it was time to talk about Sandusky. After placing the dishes in the dishwasher, Louise sat back down at the table.

"Sam, I've been praying about Sandusky. You know I'm happy here in Dubuque. You also know I love my job. Listen to me now before you say anything. Hear me out."

Sam listened intently, expecting negative words with a definite *no* at the end.

"It's hard on me. It's hard on you, and it's tearing apart our marriage. I know how much pastoring means to you, and I realize how much you're suffering inside. I know you want to pastor— possibly in Sandusky."

Sam could feel a climax coming in what Louise was going to say.

"Honey, if that's what you want—if that's going to bring you happiness, I'm willing to go. But if it doesn't work out in Sandusky, I want you to promise me you will never pursue another church. Promise me!"

Sam was stunned. Looking deep into her eyes, he could see her sincerity and love for him.

"Are you sure about this, Louise? Are you really willing to make the move with me to Sandusky?"

"Yes, Sam, I am. But are you willing to abide by my one condition? If this doesn't work out..."

"Okay! Yes! But I've got to meet with them first. Maybe it won't

116

work out. Maybe they've already hired someone else. I'll call them and see."

Both Sam and Louise got up from the table. In the middle of the kitchen, they embraced each other, ending in a tender, passionate kiss. They hadn't done much of that for a while and were elated at the warm feeling they both experienced.

Sam decided to call the church in Sandusky the next day to inquire if the position was still open.

The church secretary answered the phone. He asked her about the position. She told him the pulpit committee had not made a recommendation yet. He then asked her who to contact. She gave him the name and number of the committee chairman—Bryan Ferguson.

Sam had already sent his credentials and resume to the church. He was hoping the committee had followed up on the references in his resume. He listed all of the churches he had pastored but gave only the names and numbers of his people—those who loved and appreciated him.

Bryan Ferguson set up a weekend with Rev. Samuel Gashler, when he and Louise could travel to Sandusky and meet with the pulpit committee Saturday evening, then preach a message in the Sunday morning service.

Both Sam and Louise were excited as they drove the 468 miles from Dubuque to Sandusky. Louise was excited but apprehensive. Sam was excited with prospects of a new ministry with new opportunities.

They found Sandusky to be a charming city. Before arriving at the church, they drove around looking at all of the shopping areas, restaurants, parks, and other possibilities. They both envisioned a good life in Sandusky, Ohio.

They pulled up in front of First Church of Sandusky around five o'clock in the afternoon. Sam had informed Bryan Ferguson they would be at the church by five or a little after. Bryan and his wife, Dorothy, were already waiting for their arrival.

First Church was fairly new, with beautiful stained-glass

windows in the sanctuary. Bryan told them the windows were taken from their old building, which had been torn down in another part of town.

Bryan and Dorothy Ferguson took the Gashlers out to a fancy restaurant in town and then escorted them back to the church to meet the other four members on the pulpit committee.

The meeting was pleasant, with the usual questions being asked about education etc., although most of it was in his resume. They also asked about his vision for ministry. He told them what he had said to other pulpit committees over the years. His vision was always outreach and church growth. That always impressed the committees, although he never presented specifics.

The Saturday evening meeting went well, and the Sunday morning worship was fabulous. Sam and Louise talked about the church and community most of the way back to Dubuque the next day.

Sam knew it would be a while before he would hear from the pulpit committee at First Church. Both Sam and Louise were at peace during the waiting period. Sam was at peace, knowing he had performed well before the pulpit committee as well as in the pulpit that Sunday. Louise was at peace because she had placed the entire affair in God's hands. Secretly, a part of her wished the move wouldn't happen.

Two weeks after their trip to Sandusky, Sam received a telephone call from Bryan Ferguson.

"Hi, Rev. Gashler. This is Bryan Ferguson from First Church of Sandusky. Hey, are you still interested in being our pastor? The congregation voted to call you as our pastor."

"Sounds good to me, Bryan. I'm thrilled and excited about the opportunity to serve the church in Sandusky. I know Louise is all excited."

"Okay, well, we'll have to work out the details with you, especially moving you here. We'll pay all of your moving expenses."

"Bryan, I'll check on a moving van and send an estimate to you. Is that okay?"

"That'll be fine. Check your schedule to see when you and Louise will be arriving with your stuff. Our parsonage has been totally renovated and is awaiting your arrival."

"Okay, Bryan. I'll talk to my wife to see what she thinks about how soon we'll be ready to move."

With the conversation ended, Sam turned to his wife seated nearby in the living room. "Louise, they've decided to call me."

"Yes, I know. I overheard your conversation."

Sam was elated and was acting like he had won the lottery.

Sam and Louise figured it would take a month to give their employers fair notice and organize all of their things ready for the movers. Time went slowly for Sam, but time went by fast for Louise as she packed household items in boxes so they wouldn't get broken in transit.

Moving day came. Sam and Louise traveled to Sandusky with great anticipation of the life before them. The moving van was already in front of the parsonage as they pulled into the driveway. Church people were helping the movers unload and carry in boxes and furniture. Bryan Ferguson and Dorothy met them as they got out of their car.

"Welcome, Pastor and Louise. Welcome to your new home. May God richly bless you as you serve Him in Sandusky."

Sam was a little embarrassed by Bryan's salutation. Louise thought it was wonderful.

Their arrival was on a Monday. Sam would have to unload all of his books and office items before Sunday. A sermon would have to be prepared. Oh, how he was looking forward to standing behind the pulpit once again. Oh, how he was excited to be standing before his own congregation.

Life was good for both Rev. Samuel Gashler and Louise during the first three years of their ministry at First Church. But the fourth year was rough and controversial. A leadership crisis developed. Not everyone liked or appreciated Rev. Gashler's ministry style. Even Bryan and Dorothy Ferguson became disenchanted with

Sam's manipulation and standing on some social issues. There was obvious tension in the church.

Board meetings were especially difficult. People were complaining about his sermons. The church treasurer was upset with the amount of money he was spending or the amount of money he was asking to spend.

Several individuals sent unsigned letters to the board of elders, saying they would leave the church if something wasn't done. The big complaint was Sam's belligerence. He would not listen to or take advice.

On the other side, Sam had his admirers. They would follow him no matter what. He groomed and encouraged them. They would make great leaders under his leadership. The others, in time, would have to be forced out. He realized it wouldn't happen overnight.

# 13

# REVEREND SAMUEL GASHLER
# MEETS JESUS CHRIST

Something was happening. Sam lay on the floor of his office. His body was weak and racked with pain. He wanted Louise desperately, but he knew she was at a denominational women's conference in Detroit.

*What's happening to me?* he thought. *Oh God, help me! I don't want to die like this! Please, God, send someone.*

Sam tried to get to his feet, but the pain was too great. If he could only get to his phone to dial 911. He lay helpless on his office floor, drifting in and out of consciousness.

During this time, Sam had a vision of Jesus Christ standing before him. He could see and feel His loving, piercing eyes. The Lord said nothing, but Sam knew what He was communicating.

Sam had never felt such love. At the same time, he felt a disturbance in his soul. All of a sudden he could see the darkness of his heart—his motives and attitudes. He could feel the insincerity and lust for power radiating from his heart. It made him spiritually sick. He wanted to run—to hide from those all-knowing eyes. The sense of being totally undone washed over his soul.

It was then that Sam's family came into view. He saw the anguish and tears on Louise's face and felt her pain of being hurt.

Then his sons, Eric and Allan, stood before him. He could see the times when he should have been there for them—the games missed, the times he should have spent listening to their cares and dreams—all gone, never to be recovered.

An unbearable sense of being lost gripped his soul. Much of his life was a waste, he thought. He could see a black hole. At first he didn't know where it was or what it represented. Then it came to him it was his heart. His heart was black.

Again, he could see the beautiful and loving face of Jesus. Jesus didn't speak, but Sam knew the message. It was a message of love for him. This love transcended anything he had ever known. Sam could feel the arms of Jesus embracing him. The lostness and darkness faded away from his soul. All he knew from that point on was God's undying love for him—Samuel Gashler.

All of a sudden Sam was jolted to consciousness by the paramedics as they worked on his chest. They knew exactly what had happened to his physical body. He had a cardiac arrest. Sam had died but was brought back to life again.

Margaret Ginsberg did come to work at her exact time. She found Rev. Gashler on his office floor and called 911. This was the same lady he was going to fire later on that day.

Louise was promptly informed of Sam's heart attack and rushed home from Detroit as fast as she could. She didn't know if Sam would be alive by the time she got back to Sandusky.

Sam was placed in intensive care at the hospital. As Louise entered his room, she could see he was awake with tubes running down his throat and attachments on his arms.

He looked at Louise with new eyes. He couldn't express himself, but she sensed something was different about him. She grabbed his hand, with tears streaming down her cheeks. Sam gave a wink with a look of deep love for her.

It took a few days before Sam was out of the ICU and into a regular hospital room. The tubes were gone, but his voice was raspy.

Louise spent much of her time, day and night, in his room. She knew something was going on inside of her husband, but she didn't want to press him. She knew he would tell her when the time was right.

It took a couple of weeks before Sam was released from the hospital. He would rest at home for another month to six weeks before he would go back to work.

As soon as he was released from the hospital, Sam sat Louise down to share the whole story of what had happened to him that morning in his office—both physically and spiritually. He told her of his collapse on the floor and how painful it was to experience a heart attack. Then Sam began to tell her of his encounter with Jesus through the fog of being in and out of consciousness. She listened intently as he told her of the overpowering love he experienced. He then explained his sense of lostness and despair—the black hole he believed was his soul.

Sam talked for an hour or more, telling her how God had changed his life.

"Louise, I had an encounter with Jesus Christ. God used my heart attack to bring me to salvation. All of these years I've been preaching and pastoring without knowing Christ as my Savior. I knew theology and I knew about Christ, but I didn't really know Him as my personal Savior. But after my encounter with Him, I asked Him into my heart. I asked Him to forgive my sins. I repented of my unrighteous attitudes. Even now God is revealing to me all of the people I've hurt—especially you and the boys. God has forgiven me, but I want to ask you right now to forgive me for all the hurt I've caused you over the years. I'm so sorry for the pain. Honey, will you—can you forgive me?"

By this time Louise was sobbing happy tears in gratitude for all God had done and continued to do within Sam's heart. She had prayed for years that he would change. God was answering her prayers.

"One thing I need to do right away is reach out to Allan and Eric. I must ask for their forgiveness as well. For most of their lives, I haven't been much of a dad. It's late, but I want to reconcile with Allan. Perhaps I can be a part of his life again."

"Oh Sam, I can see Jesus in you. Before, I just saw a professional pastor—one who pursued his own interests. I saw a husband, but not one who would give warmth and love. I saw a father, but not one who would show love or understanding to his sons."

"Louise, I must go before our congregation when I'm able to share—to give my testimony. I want people to know about how God has made a difference in my life. I also need to ask for forgiveness from our leadership. I want to reconcile with those people."

"Honey, some may not forgive or want to be reconciled. The hurt may be too deep."

"I realize that, but I must try."

A look of sincere joy came across Sam's face—a look Louise had never seen before. Then Sam spoke up again. "Louise, I gave my heart and life to Jesus Christ for the first time the day of my heart attack. I repented of all my sins and invited Him into my life. My heart has been transformed, and I know His blood shed on the cross was truly for me. Before, it was a concept—an abstract concept. It was the same with His birth and resurrection. I felt that his virgin birth was a good story but probably didn't happen that way. His resurrection from the dead was an impossibility."

"But Sam, you preached some wonderful sermons on Easter Sundays about Jesus's resurrection. How could you—"

"I preached what the people could hear. I couldn't preach how I felt or what I really believed. I preached traditional messages. Some of them I used from other ministers' sermons—from books."

The Rev. Samuel Gashler, on his first Sunday back in the pulpit, gave testimony of his conversion, not sparing anything. That day many of the congregation, at the close of the service, came to the front in support of their newly converted pastor. A few were shocked and remained in their pews.

Days later Sam called all of his leadership together for an important meeting.

"Brothers and sisters, you have all heard my testimony. God is doing a work in my heart and life. I know I've hurt some of you here, and I want to say I'm sorry. Please, with all my heart, will you forgive me?"

Tears were running down his face, and all of the leaders came to Sam, embracing him. A peace settled over the entire meeting.

Sam wrote all of his previous churches a letter of testimony, explaining his conversion. Each letter asked for forgiveness from leaders in the individual churches.

Two churches wrote letters of forgiveness. One church wrote an accusing letter with a litany of Sam's abuses while at their church. The letter was typed on church stationary but was unsigned.

Sam understood their hurt and bitterness. He prayed that whoever wrote the letter would eventually find peace and forgiveness in his or her heart.

Thanksgiving was coming. Louise decided to invite Allan and Eric to travel to Sandusky for a family Thanksgiving.

The first to respond was Eric. He wrote that he and his family would be coming. They would travel from their home in Iowa City.

It took a couple of weeks before Allan wrote his letter. Yes, he also would be coming for Thanksgiving. Allan was still living in Davenport. Both Sam and Louise were thrilled.

Eric had two little girls. Dawn was five, and Erica was three. He and his wife, Helen, had married soon after their graduation from the University of Iowa. Allan was still single, with no girlfriend.

Louise prepared a fantastic meal including turkey, dressing, mashed potatoes and gravy, green beans, cranberry sauce, and pumpkin pie. Everyone enjoyed it, and everyone was stuffed following the meal.

Helen volunteered to help Louise clean up and do the dishes. Sam invited Allan and Eric to join him in his study for a talk. The sons were a little surprised by the invitation to the study. They thought a soft living room sofa or recliner would be more appropriate. After they were seated together in Sam's study, he started explaining what was on his heart.

"Eric and Allan, I have a lot to say to you. But first I want to tell you about my conversion."

"Your what, Dad?" Eric asked in surprise.

"My conversion. I have had a transformation in my heart and life. When I had my heart attack, I experienced something that's hard to explain. Jesus Christ appeared to me. I had passed out and was lying on my office floor. It was a vision of Him standing in front of me. He didn't say anything, but I knew the message. It was one of darkness, of my own sins. I could see things I had done and the people I had used. Boys, I could see what I had done to you. The baseball games I missed. The times I should have been there for you. I know there were times when you tried to tell me your problems, but I was too busy to listen. And Allan, I know I contributed to your rebellion against God and the church. You probably saw my hypocrisy."

The sons listened intently as their father continued his story of repentance, conversion, and transformation.

"I can't undo what I've done to you as you were growing up, but I promise to be a better father now."

"Since we've been here, I've noticed a real change in you," Eric said as he had observed something different about his dad. "The intensity is gone. You always seemed to be intense about something—a board meeting, a conference, or a church problem. I never felt I had your full attention, but now you're here with us and you're at peace."

"I'm at peace because I'm at peace with God for the first time in my life. I had an encounter with Jesus Christ. Boys, I truly experienced God's love and His forgiveness. It was a powerful experience. God used my heart attack to bring me to Himself."

Allan sat and listened, skeptical at first. Then he began to share his heart. "Dad, I'm tired of the hurt. I'm tired of being a rebellious son. The church always seemed like a game people played. When I was a little boy I enjoyed Sunday school, especially when Mom was my teacher. But going to church was boring and meaningless to me. I hated your sermons, and it got worse as I became a teenager. You were different at home than you were at the church. I hated the way you treated Mom.

"Dad, it's going to take me some time to take all of this in."

"Son, I know it will, and I know you have a lot to forgive in me. I want to ask both of my boys to forgive me. I want to be reconciled to you, Allan, no matter how long it may take."

"Dad," Eric said. "Dad I forgive you! I want our relationship to be close—closer than it's been the last few years."

Allan was obviously in deep contemplation. He wasn't as quick to forgive his father as was Eric. He thought, *What if this change doesn't last?*

It would take Allan time to fully forgive and become reconciled to his father.

The three men filed out of Sam's study into the living room, where Louise and Helen were settled after cleaning up the kitchen.

"Louise, I shared my conversion testimony with Eric and Allan. I asked the boys to forgive me for being a bad father. I want reconciliation with both of them. It will take time, I realize. Sharing my experience was only the first step."

Eric shared his father's story with Helen before going to bed that night. Allan continued his contemplation about his father's supposed encounter with Jesus. He was skeptical, but down deep, he wanted to believe.

It was time for Allan to leave for Davenport, Iowa, on Saturday morning following Thanksgiving.

Eric and his family left Sandusky on Monday morning. It was important for him to hear his father preach on Sunday. He could hear and feel the power—the conviction. He was moved to make a decision in his own heart to be a true disciple—to be a better husband and father.

Louise rejoiced because she had a new husband, and he was a man of God.

# ABOUT THE AUTHOR

Dennis H. Davenport has ministered through gospel music, evangelism, writing, and pastoring for 48 years. He has traveled with his wife, Joyce, throughout the United States and has gone on two mission tours to The Philippines. He is well qualified to address issues brought to light in this Christian novel.

Printed in the United States
By Bookmasters